THE
DAISY
CHAIN

AL CAMPBELL

Red Door

Published by RedDoor

www.reddoorpress.co.uk

© 2022 Al Campbell

ISBN 978-1-913062-93-4

A CIP catalogue record for this book is available from the British Library

Cover design by Clare Connie Shepherd
Daisy illustration by Fleur Campbell

Typesetting: Jen Parker, Fuzzy Flamingo
www.fuzzyflamingo.co.uk

Printed and bound in Denmark by Nørhaven

My mother, Jean Lorraine Estelle Campbell, was a woman born with humble prospects. At a time when women were little considered, like my character Daisy, she worked hard using her brain, talent and personality to defy expectations and become somebody of whom people took notice.

Throughout her life, she encouraged me to do the same.

Thanks, Mum. This book is dedicated to your memory.

And to every one of the many thousands of women like you.

THE BARBICAN

A coach-and-four drives through the arch and pulls up at the Leg O'Mutton. Tired from the long journey from Suffolk, crammed next to a fat parson and opposite a farmer with halitosis, Daisy can't wait to get out. The groom throws her bags down into the mud.

The air at the Barbican, a nexus for transport, is foetid. Having had to share a bed at the overnight inn with a widow who snored, Daisy wearily stands surrounded by the noise of animals and the smell of excrement, endeavouring to keep her boots clean. She is tall for a girl – easily tall enough to see over the withers of a good-sized cob – and what country folk would describe as 'lanky'. Even in the weak, low-elevation, morning spring light, the sun glints copper in her auburn hair, a shining contrast to her sombre mourning clothes.

As she looks around, lost and forlorn, a youth barges into her, knocks her to the cobbles, seizes one of her bags and runs off. Daisy indignantly jumps to her feet and starts to give chase.

Much to the surprise of them both, a strikingly tall and handsome man sticks out a long leg and trips the would-be thief who sprawls to the ground in a heap. The man retrieves the bag, grabs the youth by the collar from behind, pulls him to his feet and despatches him with a kick up the backside. He walks over to Daisy who is catching her breath and brushing dirt from her jacket.

'Are you all right, miss?' he asks in a deep baritone voice, whilst holding out her bag.

Noticing he speaks with a foreign accent, Daisy regards him with interest. He is strong-jawed with blue eyes and long, fair hair tied neatly with a black, silk ribbon. Despite his clothes being travel-stained, she sees he is elegantly dressed. She finds her tongue.

'Actually, sir, I am quite all right – and I would most certainly have caught him. You didn't need to involve yourself!'

The man looks at her quizzically and raises an eyebrow. Daisy takes the bag from him and remembers her manners.

'But I thank you, sir. My possessions hold no great value, but much sentiment.'

The man bows. 'Johannes Van der Humm, pleased to be of service.'

Daisy curtseys. 'Miss Daisy Salter – obliged to have received the same.'

'I assume, Miss Salter, that this is your first time at the Barbican? You will have observed it is not the best place for a young woman travelling alone.'

'I have only been through London with my father before now, sir. And then only twice.'

Van der Humm looks at her closely and realises she is wearing mourning clothes.

'Would I be correct in supposing that your father can accompany you no more?'

'Sadly, sir, he cannot.'

'My sincere condolences.' Van der Humm dips his head in respect, and Daisy nods her gratitude. 'Well, Miss Salter, I am for the inn and some lunch. My Dutch countrymen tell me that this inn, being so close to Smithfield Market, does an excellent mutton pie. Perhaps you would join me, and together we can oversee your bags?'

'In that case, you are a very kind Dutchman, sir, but first I must find which coach will take me onwards to Richmond.'

Van der Humm smiles. 'This is a happy coincidence. I am bound for Bristol on a coach that departs at three o'clock. That same coach makes a scheduled stop at Richmond to change horses. Do you have your ticket yet?'

Daisy shakes her head. 'Not as yet, sir; I still have to buy one.'

The Dutchman makes an expansive gesture with his hands. 'Happenstance, I have a ticket to spare, my intended travelling companion is unwell.' He smiles. 'Please, be my guest – firstly for mutton pie and then the coach trip.'

'That is very generous, sir, but I can pay – for both.'

Van der Humm tilts his head to one side and looks down his long and elegant nose. 'I'm sure you can, Miss Salter. But, *on both counts,* perhaps you will let a foreign gentleman be, well, gentlemanly.'

Daisy smiles and nods her acceptance. Van der Humm picks up her bags and ushers her into the inn.

They eat in companionable silence. As the serving girl

clears away her empty plate, Daisy finishes her glass of wine.

'I have to admit that I was hungry and thirsty. It was a fine mutton pie. Thank you.'

Van der Humm gives a deprecating wave of his hand. 'Do you know that you have something blue on the side of your nose?'

'Nothing but a smudge of cerulean.'

Van der Humm nods appreciatively. 'A fine hue of blue paint. You are an artist, Miss Salter?'

'Well, I paint, sir. But I am not sure I could call myself an artist.'

'And what do you paint that is blue?'

'For the most part, sir, I paint flowers. It is a hobby. The cerulean is left there from when I was painting the flowers I left on my father's grave.' She rustles in her satchel and hands him a piece of heavy paper.

He regards it with scholarly interest. '*Myosotis*?'

'Indeed, sir. Mouse ear from the original Greek. Or forget-me-nots as we more commonly know them.'

'It is beautifully done.' He returns the work. 'And very appropriate for a graveyard setting, both bright and poignant.'

'Indeed, I do hope so. I do not know when I shall see Sudbury again.'

'I too have an interest in flowers, but like many of my countrymen, my passion is the genus *Tulipa*.'

Daisy rustles in her satchel some more and brings out more paintings to hand across. 'Ah, tulips. They are most beautiful, sir. I love the bold colours, and their audacity to be so striking before rapidly fading away.'

Van de Humm looks at the paintings admiringly. 'These are not just sketches, Miss Salter. They are most accomplished. May I ask what takes you to Richmond?'

'My father having died, it has been decided I am to live with my sister.' Daisy's eyes drop, and she looks forlorn.

'From your demeanour, you are not entirely happy at the prospect, Miss Salter?'

Daisy regards him for a long second. 'As we are strangers, sir, I feel I can speak openly to you. I love my sister very much, but I cannot say the same about her husband who is a pompous brute. In some ways, I travel now to my salvation; in others, I feel I am sent to purgatory.'

Outside, a voice cries that the Bristol Coach departs in ten minutes. Van der Humm stands and gestures Daisy to do the same.

'You have my sympathies, Miss Salter. I hope it is your salvation you find, rather than the waiting room to Hell.'

RICHMOND GREEN

In an elegant Georgian drawing room, in a significant house overlooking Richmond Green, a well-dressed man in his mid-forties, not quite handsome with a cruel-looking mouth, paces up and down the carpet. Taking out his pocket watch, he opens it then scowls at a soberly dressed woman with black ribbons threaded through her golden hair. She looks almost half his age, dandling an infant on her knee.

'Whenever is that damned sister of yours going to arrive?' the man says grumpily.

The woman passes the baby to a nurse, pours tea, gives him a cup and looks up.

'She'll be well on her way, husband. She was stopping in Epping last night and coming first thing via the turnpike road as far as the Barbican where she has to change coaches.'

The man grunts.

'Why must she impose herself upon us? Especially so close to our May Ball?'

'Hugo, we have been through this before,' the woman replies despairingly. 'We have lost our father, our uncle has inherited – he will doubtless sell the estate to pay his gambling debts, and so Daisy is left with nowhere else to go.'

'She should be married so some other man can pay for her,' Hugo retorts.

'Daisy isn't the sort men naturally fall for – she's rather studious,' Fanny replies, frowning. 'Anyway, somebody had to keep house for Papa after Mama died – you wouldn't have him here!'

Hugo nearly chokes on his tea. 'Certainly not,' he splutters.

Two hours later, as the clock above the mews strikes five, the coach and four pulls up at a pair of substantial gates with the name 'Godolphin House' wrought into the ironwork. The coach door opens, Van der Humm gets out, hands Daisy down and helps the groom with her bags.

'It has been a pleasure to make your acquaintance, Miss Salter. Who knows, perhaps we will meet again one day. In the meantime, welcome to your new home.'

Van der Humm climbs back up, giving Daisy a final smile before closing the coach door behind him. With a cheery wave, the driver cracks his whip, and the horses trot off.

Daisy surveys the gates. *Home?* she wonders. *Or prison?*

Fanny is working at her embroidery when there is a knock on the door. It opens and a maid enters.

'Miss Daisy Salter, my lady,' she announces.

Fanny stands as Daisy enters. The two rush into each other's arms and exchange a huge embrace. Fanny pushes Daisy to arm's length.

'Sad times, Daisy.'

Daisy says nothing but throws her arms around Fanny again. The door bursts open, and Hugo strides in. Daisy turns towards him, curtseys and looks him in the eye.

'Hello, brother.'

Hugo steps forwards and peers closely at her.

'What's that blue on your face?'

Not enjoying Hugo being so close, Daisy takes a step back. 'Paint, I expect – I painted the forget-me-nots on Papa's grave to give to Fanny as a keepsake.'

Hugo snorts and looks her up and down. 'Such nonsense – where will painting get you? You should make more of yourself, girl, find a husband.' He walks towards the window, turns around and puts his hands behind his back – all pomp and pride. 'Now you are finally arrived, let us get things clear. You're here to look after our daughter Esme and be Fanny's companion. When I have guests, you are to stay out of the way and keep Esme out of the way. That means if we have people for lunch or dinner you will eat with the servants.'

Hugo stares at her, Daisy holds his eye. 'Yes, brother, thank you, brother.'

Hugo stomps out. Fanny takes Daisy by the arm. 'You must be exhausted; let me show you your room.'

Upstairs, Daisy looks out of the garden window. 'Fanny, I just love the formality of your garden and the layout of the planting.'

'We have our annual ball in six weeks' time. I've told the gardener everything has to be perfect – you'll find so much to paint—'

Daisy looks archly at Fanny and interrupts—'If I can find time to paint.'

'Of course, you will! And you must visit the hothouses – there are any number of plants waiting to be put out for the big day.' Fanny tilts her head to one side and smiles. 'It's so good to have you home with me.'

Daisy wanly returns the smile as Fanny turns to leave. *Home? Or prison?* Once again, the thought runs through her mind.

Fanny stops by the door. 'You must be weary. I have a maid for you, one of Hugo's blackamoors, called Kate. She will help you unpack.'

'A maid? Do I really need my own servant?'

Fanny looks exasperated and adopts a bossy tone as she sweeps out of the room. 'Good heavens, Daisy, you're not in the country now – this is polite society, and you had better get used to it.'

Sitting on the bed, Daisy realises just how tired she is and lies back, staring vacantly at the high ornate ceiling. There is a knock, and Kate, a handsome woman in her late twenties with skin as black as night, enters. She coughs quietly and enquires solicitously, 'Is anything wrong, miss?'

Daisy sees the concern in Kate's eyes. 'I've had a long journey, that's all.'

Kate points to Daisy's bags. 'I'll unpack those for you later. Lady Fanny tells me you're an artist?'

Daisy nods.

'Well, miss, I have drawn something to welcome you to Godolphin House.'

'You've drawn something – that's very kind. What is it?'

Kate's smile lights up the room. 'A bath, miss, I've drawn you a bath!'

Daisy suddenly relaxes and chuckles. 'Now that is something I cannot wait to see.'

A week or two passes. Daisy slips into a routine of looking after Esme, accompanying Fanny around Richmond and, most days, finding an hour or two to paint. Thus occupied, one sunny morning whilst Esme naps, Fanny finds her in the garden painting wallflowers. Daisy looks up as Fanny peers over her shoulder.

'Don't you just love wallflowers, Fanny? So colourful, so proud, so free.'

Fanny murmurs her approval. 'I have an idea. If you would be willing to let me have two wallflower paintings, I will ask Hugo to get them framed. We have hanging space in the entrance hallway – wallflowers will fit the bill perfectly!'

'Naturally. Although I don't think Hugo has much respect for my work.'

'Don't worry. I know how to be nice to him when I want something.'

'You always were the clever one when it came to men.'

Fanny regards her circumspectly. 'It's a skill you could do with learning.'

Daisy looks disingenuous. 'I shall work on my portraiture skills.'

Fanny harrumphs. 'That wasn't what I meant, and you know it! Anyway, have you been to the hothouses yet? There's a lot there to paint.' With a nod in their direction, she strolls back towards the house.

With Fanny gone, Daisy picks up her paints and brushes, and heads deeper into the garden towards an array of glass roofs. She wanders into a large greenhouse where a black man is fussing over plants on a bench. He looks up as she enters and bobs his head.

'Good morning, miss.' He has a deep and resonant voice.

'Hello. I'm Miss Salter, Lady Fanny's sister,' Daisy tells him.

'Yes, miss, I know.'

'What is that plant you have there? I haven't seen the like before.'

'It is a melon, miss. Lord Hugo is fiercely fond of a melon, yet I struggle to propagate them.'

Daisy walks over and takes a closer look. 'What's your name?' she asks.

'Gardner, miss.'

Daisy looks at him slightly sternly. 'Well, I can see you're a gardener, but what is your name?'

'My name *is* Gardner, miss. My father was Lord Hugo's gardener in the colonies. The name stuck. Sadly, my father was the one who had the gift of growing melons. I can make most things grow, but melons seem to evade me somehow.'

Daisy looks closer. 'Hmm, Mr Gardner, it seems to me you might be in need of a paintbrush.'

Gardner regards her curiously. 'I have heard you are a painter, miss, but with no melon to paint, I don't see what a paintbrush might do?'

Meanwhile, Daisy has been searching through her painting kit and brings out a range of paintbrushes of varying sizes, looking at them closely, trying to select one.

'The thing is, Mr Gardner, I believe that, if I were to insert a paintbrush into the male flower and tickle it a little then take it out and brush the female flower with it, your melons might pollinate and give you fruit.' She eyes up several brushes. 'Do you think, Mr Gardner, that size matters?'

'I've no idea, miss; best I leave an expert like you to decide that.'

Daisy selects a brush and demonstrates to Gardner what to do then hands him the brush so he can try for himself. Gardener takes the brush nervously.

'Do you not think, Mr Gardner, that such an act might benefit from some sort of benediction?'

Gardner looks thoughtful. 'Well, miss, my father used to bless every seed he sowed with a few words.'

Daisy looks at him expectantly.

Gardner inserts the brush into a flower. 'God speed the seed with Mother Nature's love,' he intones.

Later that evening, Kate is brushing Daisy's long, auburn tresses. 'Excuse me, miss, but I saw Lady Fanny showing Master Hugo two of your paintings today.'

'Well, Kate, I don't expect you to tell me he was impressed.'

'To be honest, miss, he hardly took any notice. But I saw them, miss, and I thought they were wonderful. So delicate and exact that I felt I could reach out and touch them and smell them. I wouldn't worry about what Master Hugo says – your paintings speak for themselves.'

Daisy studies Kate in her mirror. 'That is an astute perception. Tell me, Kate, how do you come to be at Godolphin House?'

Kate stops brushing. 'I'm one of Master Hugo's slaves, miss. He brought me to England from one of his plantations in the colonies, where I was bred and grew up.'

Daisy turns around and stares at her. 'I didn't know Lord Hugo had estates overseas.'

'Yes, miss, tobacco in Virginia and cotton further south in the Carolinas.'

'And you are not here of your own free will?'

'Slaves have no free will, miss. All of the staff here are slaves brought across the ocean. Why wouldn't we be? I am a slave as my mother was a slave and my grandmother before her – although she was owned by Master Hugo's father. You could say that slavery runs in the family.'

Daisy looks thoughtful as the pair share a silent moment. 'So, you are here enslaved, and I am here entrapped.'

Kate moves around and resumes brushing Daisy's hair. 'It's not all bad, miss. I'd rather be here than on the plantations where to be a black woman is to be available to any white man. Now I'm older, even the Master doesn't bother to touch me.'

Daisy stands up, shocked. 'Lord Hugo made advances on you?'

'More than advances, miss. Especially on the journey from Virginia to England. But I am his property – he can do with me as he wishes.'

'Does Lady Fanny know?'

'I have no idea, miss. If she does, she may well, like many women, turn a blind eye to it. Knowing the Master as I do'—Kate's eyes slide sideways as if clouded by a bad memory—'I would say he is neither a gentleman, nor a gentle man, when it comes to the bedroom.'

'Do you ever wish you could be free, Kate? I do.'

'That seems most unlikely in my case, miss, although I understand there is a Member of Parliament called William Wilberforce who is hoping to present a bill of emancipation.'

Daisy is taken aback. 'Goodness, Kate, how do you know these things?'

'I read *The Gazette*, miss. Don't you?'

'Yes, but I did not suppose you could read.'

'My father taught me, miss. He was our preacher on the plantation, and I learned by reading the *Bible*.'

'Surely, if you have had a Christian education, you must feel even more inclined to escape?'

'What would be the point – I have nowhere to go. I get fed here, and I have a good mistress.'

'Yes, Fanny is a kind-hearted soul.'

Kate stops brushing and smiles at Daisy. 'I wasn't talking about her ladyship, miss.'

Some days later, at breakfast, a footman brings in two packages. He gives them to Fanny who rips them open. They are Daisy's wallflower paintings, now beautifully framed. The two women regard them with delight. Daisy gives Hugo a rare smile.

'Thank you, brother, this is most kind of you.'

'Waste of time, money and wall space. Now pass me the kedgeree. And Daisy, you are far too familiar with that maid of yours. Maintain some propriety.'

'Propriety, brother, whatever do you mean?'

'She's a servant.'

'Don't you mean slave, brother?'

Hugo sneers. 'Amounts to the same thing.'

THE MAY BALL

One warm summer's morning, Fanny and Daisy sit on the patio under a rose-covered pergola. Both women are out of mourning. Fanny looks glamorous and every part the lady – tumbling blonde locks and bright blue satin that matches her eyes. Daisy looks rather more homespun.

'Daisy, I must send out invitations for the ball. Would you paint a flower on each to make them more enticing?

'Of course. Perhaps a forget-me-not? That would seem appropriate.'

'Perfect. I won't make a point of it in front of Hugo, but you must come.'

Daisy raises an eyebrow. 'How will you get away with that? You know his views about me not being around guests.'

Fanny looks resigned. 'I suppose I will have to be nice to him again.'

Daisy giggles. 'That, sister, will be twice in this same month!'

Fanny gives Daisy an old-fashioned look. 'That's quite enough, Daisy... Take that as you will. Anyway, I will make sure to invite some eligible young men.'

Daisy sits up, stiffens her back and looks Fanny in the eye. 'Darling sister, I'm not looking for a husband. Papa was my man in a million.'

Fanny reaches out and holds Daisy's hand. 'What is it that you are looking for exactly?'

'You took after Mama – you were made to marry. I just want to be me, Daisy, not Mrs Somebody Else. I learned so much from Papa. I may be a country girl, but I believe myself to be a woman of science, and I want to continue learning.' Daisy walks to the door. 'And to be allowed to know things and to use the things I have learned without a man getting in the way. Yet what are my chances of finding a husband who will let me? If I had a fortune, I wouldn't marry at all, I'd explore the world and paint the flowers I discovered.'

The two stare at each other in silence, full of sisterly affection, neither understanding the other's point of view.

Daisy breaks the silence. 'Besides, do not worry about the ball – I have nothing to wear, and I would not like to conflict with Lord Hugo's sense of propriety!'

Fanny bridles. 'You *shall* come to the ball – I will lend you one of my dresses.'

Daisy gestures to Fanny's womanly curves. 'You, sister, have a figure to make men swoon.' She gestures to her own body. 'I, on the other hand, have a body men don't even have to sway to get around. Any dress of yours would fit me nearly twice over!'

The women look at each other, then burst into fits of giggles.

'In that case, dearest sister, you will have to apply that fine scientific brain to needle and thread, and nip and tuck until you have something that fits your scrawny figure. In the meantime, I will get my corsetiere to visit. Let us see if she can create something that might push and shove that scrawny figure into a more womanly shape!'

It is the night of the ball. Daisy, in a leaf green dress that fits her perfectly, regards herself in the mirror. Kate, on her knees, puts final stitches into the hem before standing up, holding Daisy by the shoulders and turning her around to view her from all angles.

'Miss, you look as perfect as one of your paintings.'

'Thank you. I couldn't have done this without your help.'

'We all have our talents, miss. Yours is making people look closely at flowers. Mine is making sure people do not look too closely at dresses!'

'In that case, Kate, your talent is the more clandestine.'

'Clandestine, miss?'

'Secretive, Kate. Keeping things hidden.'

'I'm not sure that's entirely true, miss.' She motions to Daisy to push her breasts a little higher under her corset. 'But if true, then all women should be clandestine. Wouldn't do at all to let men know what we're thinking. Or even that we *are* thinking!'

Daisy raises an inquisitive eyebrow.

'Miss, if ever an intelligent man got to thinking about what a woman might be thinking about, he'd think little or nothing about how thoughtful a thoughtful woman could be, or what thoughts she might think!'

Daisy looks surprised. 'Well, Kate, there's a thought or four!'

Daisy, with Kate in attendance, goes downstairs and joins the party. There is music, and people are milling around. Hugo and Fanny are greeting guests in the hallway. Not knowing anybody, and without Fanny there to introduce her, Daisy stands alone regarding the dancers.

'It seems to me, Kate, that London is full of preening men and primped women.'

'Did you not dance when you lived in the country, miss?'

'After my mother passed away, we kept our own company. Although Lady Fanny would sometimes play mother's piano whilst I danced with my father.'

'You look wistful, miss.'

'He was a rather wonderful man.'

'My father too, miss.'

Daisy smiles at her sympathetically as one dance ends, people change partners, the orchestra strikes up a new air, and the gaiety and revelry continue.

'Has nobody marked your dance card, miss?'

Daisy confidentially shows Kate her empty card. 'Luckily not, as yet.' She sets her jaw and makes a decision. 'There may be wallflowers hanging in the hallway, Kate, but it seems that I am the biggest one of all. Should any gentleman want to dance attendance on me, he will need to find me in the garden.' With Kate in tow, Daisy slips out of the double doors, open to let the mild spring air into the ballroom, and on to the patio.

Unaware of Daisy's escape from the party, Hugo and Fanny stand beneath her wallflower paintings, preparing to join the guests. They are caught unawares as the butler ushers in two more guests.

Fanny looks startled. 'Hugo, it's Joseph Banks!'

Hugo turns to Fanny. 'Joseph Banks? I knew you invited him, but I didn't expect him to attend!'

Fanny looks equally bemused. 'Nor I, husband. We are honoured – he is one of the most celebrated men in England, only recently returned from his famous three-year voyage with Captain Cook on HMS *Endeavour*.'

For once, Hugo looks impressed with his wife's knowledge. 'Yes, I hear he helped plot the transit of Venus, visited New Zealand and claimed Australia for King George.'

Fanny is quite surprised by Hugo's knowledge and interest. 'I invited him because he has moved to Kew. He has brought back thousands of botanical specimens to England and been made Director of Kew Gardens.'

The footman announces Banks and his companion. 'My lord, Mr Joseph Banks and Mr Rupert Fitzgerald.'

'Mr Banks, we are honoured by your company,' says Hugo obsequiously.

Banks is a man of twenty-eight – well-dressed but not smartly. He has bushy eyebrows, a large nose, an unruly mop of hair, a natural confidence and a commanding manner. His companion, Fitzgerald, is younger and taller, red-haired and more fashionably dressed, but not foppish.

The pair bow politely to Hugo and Fanny.

'Thank you, Sir Hugo, Lady Godolphin, for your kind invitation. The moment I received it I simply had to attend.'

Fanny smiles, delighted. 'Mr Banks, we expected you to be too busy, so shortly returned from your great adventures.'

'It was a long trip, but we are never too busy to seek out new scientific talent.'

Hugo and Fanny look bemused.

Rupert joins the conversation. 'Mr Banks is referring to the painting on the invitation, Lady Godolphin.'

Banks points to the paintings of the wallflowers. 'And, if I'm not mistaken, the same hand is responsible for those fine works.'

Hugo waves a deprecating hand. 'Just some nonsense my wife liked – nothing of merit.'

Banks looks at Hugo curiously. 'On the contrary, they are remarkably exact representations of *Erysimum cheiri*.' He turns to Fanny. 'Members of the brassica family, you know – cabbages and the like – you cannot eat them, but so colourful.'

The nuance of the conversation has completely bypassed Hugo who looks on with a vague expression.

Rupert is equally enthused. 'The painting is so elegantly descriptive, but also botanically correct, like the *Myosotis* painted on the invitation.' He turns to Fanny who is slightly perplexed by the Latin. 'Did you paint them, Lady Godolphin, the forget-me-nots?'

Fanny now understands. 'No, sir, it is my sister's work.'

Banks and Rupert look at each other, slightly

disappointed. Banks speaks. 'We had hoped to find her here.'

Fanny brightens. 'Oh, she is here, sir.' She looks around and sees Kate vanishing through the patio doors. 'I imagine, sir, that she will be in the garden.'

Banks beams. 'Of course, where else?'

Fanny points towards the terrace. 'Gentlemen, let me show you the way.'

Daisy is so intently inspecting a flower, she doesn't hear them until Fanny gives a gentle cough. She jumps and turns around.

'Here are two gentlemen who would talk with you. Mr Joseph Banks and Mr Rupert Fitzgerald, who are near neighbours of ours from Kew. Gentlemen, my sister, Miss Daisy Salter.'

The men bow politely, Daisy curtseys. Banks points at the plant that had captivated Daisy's attention just a moment before.

'Are you fond of a fuchsia, Miss Salter? You were regarding it very keenly.'

'Fuchsia, sir? I believe it is a peony.'

Banks looks pensive. 'I have been overseas and perhaps forgotten.' He points elsewhere. 'Personally, I am a great fan of those *Alcea* – foxgloves as they are known.'

Daisy is not sure whether she is being duped. 'Foxgloves indeed, sir, but the correct Latin name is *Digitalis*.' She points at a different flower. 'That is an *Alcea*, usually called a hollyhock!'

Rupert chuckles. 'Mr Banks is teasing, Miss Salter, for he is a most expert plantsman – one in fact who has many plants named after him.'

Daisy smiles politely, bemused.

Banks makes a deprecating gesture. 'That's as maybe. The truth, Miss Salter, is that I have indeed been overseas and just returned from the southern continents where I collected a great number of plants for the King's gardens at Kew. Now I need help recording and documenting them.'

'What Mr Banks is trying to ask,' Rupert continues, 'is if you would be prepared to come to Kew and spend some time painting the specimens for our records?'

Daisy blushes slightly. 'Me, sir? I am but an amateur and a woman.'

Banks looks amazed. 'I don't see how your gender comes into it, Miss Salter. Amateur or not, you show great skill in botanical representation, and Kew will be happy to pay for such skill.'

Daisy's eyes widen at the prospect. 'I'm not sure I can accept payment, sir.'

'Why ever not? I had a painter with me for the three years of my voyage – Sydney Parkinson. He was happily paid; it's not the person that is rewarded, but the skill.'

'But he does not paint for you now, sir?'

Banks' eyes cloud. 'Sadly, he died of the flux off the Cape Peninsula. We were only weeks from home.'

Fanny has been looking on silently. 'Oh, that is so very sad.'

Banks looks wistful. 'The pursuit of scientific advancement is not without risk. But Miss Salter, I can guarantee a rather safer adventure at Kew. Shall I send a carriage for you in the morning?'

Before Daisy can reply, Fanny answers, 'I'm sure that will be fine, Mr Banks.'

Banks and Rupert bow politely to both women. Fanny seizes the opportunity. 'Gentlemen, will you not stay a while and join the dancing?'

Banks sees from Rupert's expression that he would like to stay. 'We cannot stay long, my lady, but I finally have my land legs back, so it would be an honour to claim a dance with you, with your permission, of course.'

Fanny looks delighted to be asked to dance by England's most eminent scientist. 'It would be a pleasure, Mr Banks. And perhaps young Mr Fitzgerald might like to accompany Miss Salter onto the dance floor?'

Rupert colours slightly but is evidently happy at the suggestion, bowing deeply to Daisy. 'Miss Salter, would you dance with me?' He offers his arm.

Daisy sees she has been outmanoeuvred by her sister and accepts the inevitable, putting her hand on Rupert's arm. 'Thank you, Mr Fitzgerald, it is most kind of you to ask, but I have to warn you, I am not the most adept of partners.'

Rupert grins. 'In that case we will stumble through the measures together.' Daisy can't help but grin back.

Sometime later, after Banks and Rupert have left the party, the sisters take a turn in the garden, arm-in-arm, to cool off. 'I have to say, Daisy, that your Mr Fitzgerald stumbles rather well. I would go as far as to say he seemed something of an expert.'

Daisy looks sideways at her sibling. 'He is not *my* Mr Fitzgerald! Although I must admit he made everything seem rather easy.' She turns to face Fanny. 'Sister, do you not think we should ask Hugo's permission for me to go to Kew?'

Fanny gives Daisy an appraising look. 'I may be committed here for life, but there is a lot more to the world than Godolphin House. Leave Hugo to me.'

'You'll be "nice" to him?'

Fanny puts a hand on Daisy's shoulder. 'With any luck, he'll have drunk so much I won't need to be.'

At breakfast the next day, Hugo is clearly nursing a hangover.

'Husband, Daisy will be going out today. Mr Banks has asked her to go to Kew Gardens and paint some flowers for him.'

Hugo puts down the forkful of kidneys that was halfway to his mouth and glares. 'Paint flowers? That's preposterous. No, I forbid it. Anyway, I need the carriage.' He fills his mouth, starts chewing and looks down at his paper.

Daisy's bottom lip starts to tremble, and she looks at Fanny. Just then, the door opens, and a footman enters.

'There is a carriage outside, Sir Hugo, bearing the royal coat of arms and an equerry saying he is to collect Miss Salter.'

Hugo almost chokes on the kidneys.

Fanny stifles a laugh. 'Well, husband, it seems my sister has received a royal summons.' She waves airily to Daisy. 'Off you go, it doesn't do to keep royalty waiting.'

'Well then, I must go and change my clothes. I'll need my painting pockets!'

Whilst Fanny looks bemused, Daisy scampers from the room, to appear a few moments later in a voluminous dress with copious pockets bulging with brushes and sundry accoutrements.

KEW

After a drive of little more than ten minutes, the carriage swings through the gates of Kew. A footman helps Daisy down and takes care of her easel and paints. She looks around in wonder – it is a magnificent scene with gardeners busy everywhere, carrying plants, digging, planting, tending to borders, clipping the extensive lawns. A voice with a distinctive Scottish burr comes from behind.

'It makes a big impression, does it not?'

Daisy turns around, realises her mouth is open, shuts it and nods before finally managing to speak.

'Yes, indeed it does, Mr... err...?'

'Francis Masson.' The man bows. He is in his mid-thirties with thinning hair, plainly dressed. 'I am one of the senior gardeners here and recently made Mr Banks' Chief Plant Hunter.'

Daisy bobs a curtsey. 'It is a pleasure to meet you Mr Masson. Plant hunting sounds very adventurous – where do you hunt?'

'I am currently planning an expedition to the Cape. I sail in the early autumn here to arrive for late spring in the southern hemisphere, when the plants and flowers will be in their glory.'

Daisy regards Masson with more interest.

'But first, we have to document and record the specimens Mr Banks brought us back from his last trip.'

'Yes. Mr Banks suggested I might be of some help – but I'm not sure how?'

Masson indicates a path that leads towards an elegant Georgian building covered in wisteria. The pair walk towards it, gravel scrunching under their feet. Masson has a long stride, and Daisy has to walk quickly to keep up whilst he explains.

'We record all the specimens on paper, so that if anything should happen to said specimens, we have an accurate botanical record for posterity.'

'Do many perish?'

Masson points to the glasshouses behind a bank of trees. 'We have magnificent greenhouses and a very experienced team of experts. We can replicate the conditions the plants were found in and care for them well – but we do lose a few.'

Arriving at the building, Masson opens a large door and takes Daisy along a hallway to a smaller door, which he gestures for Daisy to open. She enters and catches her breath. The room is large with a domed and glazed atrium, under which sits an enormous workbench, upon which are arranged specimens of the most fantastic tropical plants. Daisy regards them, one at a time, then turns to Masson.

'Mr Masson, these are magnificent, yet I do not recognise any of them. What are they called?'

'I'm afraid I cannot tell you.'

'Is it a secret?'

'Not at all, they are not yet named. We have a small committee that meets to decide what the newly discovered plants should be called, and these are the next to be determined.'

Daisy's eyes sparkle. 'How exciting it must be to name a plant! And they are all from overseas?'

'Indeed. Brought back by Mr Banks from his voyage on HMS *Endeavour*.'

Daisy regards the plants afresh.

'Actually, Miss Salter, you are amongst no more than a dozen people in England to have seen them.'

Daisy claps her hands delightedly. At that moment, Banks enters.

'Mr Banks, thank you so much for inviting me. It is almost too exciting.'

Banks smiles boyishly. 'I too find them exciting. But I hope you are not too excited to paint them?'

'You would trust me to do that?'

'You have a great eye for botanical art. We need to keep accurate records, so we know if new finds are, well, new in the truest sense of the word or if they're a different genus, or perhaps a relative of one we already know.'

'It sounds rather technical, sir, and I have no great formal knowledge—'

'Oh, don't worry about that. We have botanists who do all that sort of thing – Francis here, or Rupert Fitzgerald. They have the expertise.'

Masson looks modest. 'But not your talent, miss.'

The three stand in companionable silence, surrounded by nature in all her glory.

Daisy walks around the table, touching the plants, stroking the leaves. 'If you're sure, I could do a couple of sketches for you to consider. When would you like me to start?'

Banks looks at Masson who sets his head to one side and nods.

'If this room is to your liking, why not start now?' Masson says in his gentle voice.

Daisy walks to the window, looks up at the sun, takes a few paces and stops.

'If I could have a table set up here for the subject, then another here for my paints and brushes – yes, I think that would be perfect.'

The men once again exchange looks – Banks raises an eyebrow. 'I see you are an artist who knows exactly what she wants.'

Daisy's back stiffens a little. 'An artist certainly, but one who thinks like a scientist. Having experimented hundreds of times with how light catches a plant, and the way to show a specimen to its best advantage, I feel confident in my analysis. My father taught me it is the ability to repeat an experiment and get the same result every time that is proof the science works.'

'Then your father has the right of it.' Banks turns to Masson. 'Francis, can you see to Miss Salter's requests?'

When Masson has gone, Banks turns to Daisy. 'That just leaves the matter of your reimbursement.'

'Sir, nobody has ever paid me for my paintings, so

I have no idea of their worth. I think I would prefer to produce a couple of pieces today so you can make your own judgement.'

Men enter with tables. Daisy immediately starts giving them directions. Banks realises that he is in the way.

'Well, Miss Salter, until this afternoon then.'

THE PAGODA

Daisy quickly finds the best light to position her easel. She settles down and starts painting. She doesn't sketch in pencil first but confidently applies the watercolour onto the thick heavy paper. She works on two paintings simultaneously. One, a brightly coloured succulent with a large, deep-red flower and dark green fleshy leaves. The other, tall and airy with long, thin stalks and a froth of small, white flowers at its crown.

She alternates between paintings, allowing the colours to soak in and dry. The window is open, but she concentrates so hard she doesn't hear the blackbird singing outside, nor the clock strike ten and then eleven. As it strikes twelve, there is a knock at the door. Rupert Fitzgerald enters, bearing a tray of food and wine.

'Good day, Miss Salter. Mr Banks suggested I might bring you some lunch.' He carefully makes space on the end of the workbench, making sure not to disturb anything important.

Daisy stretches and moves to the bench. Rupert steps across towards Daisy's paintings.

'Do you mind if I look at your work in progress, Miss Salter?' Daisy nods her agreement. Rupert studies the paintings then looks up, clearly impressed. 'I must say, they already fire the imagination.'

'That is most kind, Mr Fitzgerald. But as we are of a similar age, do you think it would be easier for us to call each other by our Christian names?'

'Why not? Mine is Rupert.' He bows.

'And mine is Daisy.' She bobs a curtsey. 'But let me tell you, Rupert, that my paintings are not intended to "fire the imagination". They are there to be an exact and accurate representation of the individual specimens.'

Rupert looks taken aback.

'There is much detail to be added – my intention is that there should be nothing there for the eye to guess at. That detail will appear after lunch. Now, what's on your tray? I'm starving!'

She breaks into a grin; Rupert grins back, and they sit down to eat and drink. Daisy is quiet for a moment, but her curiosity is killing her.

'So, Rupert, if you know Mr Banks, you must know all about Kew Gardens, whereas I know nothing. I want to hear it all, tell me everything.'

Rupert needs no encouragement to expound on his favourite topic. 'Kew Gardens belongs to King George. And Mr Banks, who takes the role of director, is the closest thing we have to a Royal Gardener. Daisy, he is the most important plantsman in the country, if not in Europe. Kew is spectacular, and Banks is Kew!'

'But he's quite recently come to work here? He didn't start Kew.'

'Quite right. Kew was started by Frederick, Prince of

Wales, with his young wife Augusta. Both worked on it together, even going so far as planting out the flower beds. Sadly, Frederick died at the turn of the half century… although Augusta took some comfort from the Earl of Bute'—Daisy looks shocked—'a plantsman of note, who kept a house on Kew Green so as to be near to Augusta. He saw the grounds re-landscaped and trees replanted. But King George and Bute never got on, and the King took responsibility for the garden when his mother became ill. He appointed Mr Banks to the position following his famous journey with Captain Cook.'

Daisy wipes her mouth with a napkin. 'I must say the gardens are a great adventure.'

Rupert drains his glass. 'Have you seen the Pagoda?'

'The Pagoda. What sort of plant is that?'

Rupert stands and beckons Daisy towards the door. 'Come and see!'

Rupert escorts Daisy down a path, pointing out flowers he correctly presumes she doesn't yet know. They come to a curve in the path, and Rupert stops. 'Put your hands over your eyes.'

Daisy does as she's told. Rupert takes her by the shoulders and turns her to face the famous Great Pagoda. 'Look now!'

Daisy takes her hands away and squeals with delight. 'What on earth is it?'

Rupert, prone to proud posturing when showing off his knowledge, strikes a rather didactic pose. 'A copy of the architecture for formal gardens in China. I hope to go one day and see for myself. It was built as a gift for

Princess Augusta by Sir William Chambers.'

The pair stand in companionable silence, slightly awestruck by the remarkable size and shape of the edifice.

'Daisy, I must get back to my work – can you find your way back to your studio?'

'Of course, I can,' came the confident reply.

'Perhaps tomorrow, you will come and see where I and the other botanists are cataloguing specimens?'

'If Mr Banks invites me back tomorrow, I would love that. Thank you for sharing so much with me today.'

Rupert bows, turns and strides off. Daisy tries retracing her steps but cannot find her way. Luckily, she spies a woman busy dead-heading roses outside of a rather lovely cottage.

Daisy gives a polite cough. 'Umm, excuse me?'

The woman stands, puts her hands on her back, and Daisy sees she is pregnant. She is quite striking with a darkish complexion and slightly African features. She sighs and adjusts her body. 'Hello. Can I help you?' The woman has a clipped, throaty accent.

'I seem to be lost.'

'Your first time in the gardens?'

'Yes. I have come to paint specimens for Mr Banks. But I went to see the Pagoda, and I cannot find my way back to my studio.'

'Ahh, then you must be Daisy. Mr Banks told me you might be joining us here.'

Daisy looks slightly discombobulated that the woman knows who she is.

'Don't worry, my dear. Mr Banks tells me everything.

We take tea together most afternoons to talk about the garden – why don't you come and join us at four o'clock?'

Daisy looks surprised by the invitation. 'That's very kind – providing Mr Banks won't mind.'

'Oh, I think he'll be fine, my dear.'

'Tea here? Is this your cottage?'

'Yes, my dear. Perhaps I should send somebody to show you the way, so you don't get lost again.'

Daisy looks relieved. 'That would be kind. Thank you. Could you tell me the way back to my studio please?'

'Follow the main path, then turn right when you come to the big *Gunnera* plant. You know what *Gunnera* looks like?'

'My father had a specimen by our mill pond.' Momentarily, Daisy remembers swinging over the enormous leaves on the seat her father had strung from a bough of the old chestnut. She makes to go then turns back. 'Would you know if anybody at Kew has a caliper I could borrow?'

'Caliper? Do you have a bad leg?'

'Not at all.'

'Well, Daisy, I don't know of anybody. But Mr Banks might. We can ask him at tea.'

Daisy walks off. The woman calls after her. 'Bring a painting to show us!'

Later that afternoon, Daisy is putting the finishing touches to a painting using a single-haired brush to make tiny, fine marks. She puts her brush down and blows the paint dry.

There is a crunch on the gravel outside, and Masson's face appears at the window. He gestures for Daisy to turn her work around and show him.

His face lights up. 'Painted with the eyes of youth. An exact likeness.'

Daisy gives a tired smile. 'Thank you, Mr Masson. I hope it will pass the test.'

Masson gives a reassuring nod. 'Will it be convenient to escort you home at half past four?'

Daisy goes to say yes, then remembers. 'Could it be a little later? I'm invited to tea at four o'clock.'

Masson smiles. 'You make friends quickly, Miss Salter.'

'We're not friends yet. I got lost and came across a lady of whom I asked directions. She invited me to tea with her and Mr Banks.'

'Was she elegant and in her thirties?'

Daisy considers for a second. 'I would say "comely".'

'Comely – hmm. And would you say she was with child?'

'Mr Masson, you know her too! Are you coming to tea?'

'Not today, Miss Salter. I can tell you, however, that most days at four, Mr Banks takes tea with Her Majesty Queen Charlotte in her cottage. You too, today, it seems.'

'That was the Queen?' Daisy looks distraught. She paces the room, puts her face in her hands, looks at Masson, walks away again, sits down with a thump and regards Masson with anguish.

Masson is amused. 'That would have been the Queen.'

'She told me to turn left by that magnificent *Gunnera*.'

'I think it would have been right?'

'Right? Right – I mean, yes.'

'Miss Salter, on the basis you have been summoned to a royal tea party, I can only wait on your convenience as regards the time at which I will escort you home. I will see you later.' Masson bows. Daisy sits down looking nervous.

At ten minutes to four, a liveried footman arrives to escort Daisy to tea. He insists on carrying her portfolio. Daisy, not used to being waited-on, follows him in procession as they walk up to the cottage door. There, the first footman hands the portfolio to a second who, in turn, ushers Daisy into the Queen's parlour where the Queen and Banks are having tea. Banks stands.

'Your Majesty, may I introduce Miss Daisy Salter?'

Daisy makes her very best obeisance then looks nervously at the floor.

'Do sit down, dear. Actually, Joseph, Daisy and I have already met… informally, so to speak.'

Daisy perches on the edge of a sofa. 'Your Majesty, I apologise. I did not know who you were.'

Banks looks on, perplexed.

'Why on earth should you? I must have looked like any other pregnant woman pruning her roses.' She pours a cup of tea and passes it across. 'Now, show us what's in your portfolio.'

Daisy passes the paintings. The Queen and Banks regard them silently. The Queen lets out a sigh.

'How I wish I could paint like this.'

Banks nods in appreciation.

Daisy's shoulders relax with relief. 'But you could, Your Majesty. It is quite simple to learn.'

'Now there's a thought. Perhaps you could teach me?'

'Oh, well, Your Majesty, I didn't mean that. I couldn't presume—'

Seeing her discomfort, Banks leans forwards. 'Miss Salter, how did you learn? Who was your teacher?'

'Oh, I just learned from a neighbour – a Mr Gainsborough.'

The Queen and Banks exchange startled looks. Banks speaks first. 'Not Thomas Gainsborough?'

'Yes, his daughters, Mary and Meg, were my best friends. Our families were neighbours in Sudbury. I used to go to his studio when he was painting their portraits and help with his paints and brushes.'

The Queen chuckles. 'And did he give you lessons?'

Daisy thinks. 'I sort of just picked up how to do it, but I suppose he did. His mother painted flowers – that was how he learned.'

The Queen moves her weight to be more comfortable. 'Well, that is a surprise – I am considering asking Mr Gainsborough to come and paint the King, myself and all of the children.'

Daisy jumps in to champion her mentor. 'He'd do an excellent job, Your Majesty.'

'Just as I'm sure you will do a good job teaching me, Daisy. Mr Banks, will you be able to spare her for a little time each day?'

'As you wish, Your Majesty.'

'Then it is agreed.' She pats her belly. 'It will keep me

occupied during the latter days of my confinement.'

Banks bows. 'If Your Majesty is happy'—he makes an open gesture that embraces Daisy—'then we are happy.'

The Queen considers. 'You know I have ladies in waiting. But I have never, until now, had a "lady in painting"! In which case, you shall call me, Ma'am.'

Daisy looks dumbstruck. Banks breaks the silence. 'For my part, Your Majesty, Kew has never had a Painter in Residence – but, if Your Majesty agrees, on the basis of the two paintings we have just seen, I think we have just found our first one.'

The Queen nods and looks Daisy squarely in the eye. 'Perhaps you would like to sleep on it, my dear, then you can let Mr Banks know tomorrow what you decide? Now, off you go, we have other things to discuss.'

Daisy, speechless, stands, curtseys and leaves the room.

'If I might venture, Your Majesty, there is more to that young woman than meets the eye.'

'She is not only delightful, Mr Banks, but interesting, unlike so many of today's coquettish girls. I suspect she may even have opinions!'

'Quite so, Your Majesty.' Banks bows and turns to leave. As he gets to the door, the Queen speaks.

'I forgot to mention that Daisy is looking for a caliper.'

'Does she have a bad leg, Your Majesty?'

'Apparently not.'

'I'll see what it is she wants it for.'

Outside, Daisy walks to a waiting carriage at the gates of Kew. Rather than Masson, she is surprised when it is Rupert who gets out.

'Mr Masson has had to go into London to meet a gentleman called Fortnum to discuss provisions for his expedition. He asked me to accompany you home.'

Rupert hands her up into the coach and climbs in after her. 'So, tell me, Daisy, was it the sort of day you expected?'

As Hugo and Fanny had guests for dinner, Daisy eats supper below stairs and goes early to her room, exhausted by the events of the day. She is sitting in her nightclothes in front of the mirror, with Kate brushing her hair, when Fanny knocks on the door, comes in and plonks herself on the bed.

'Hugo's guests are so boring. Cheer me up, sister – did you have the sort of exciting day you expected?'

Daisy feigns a slightly hurt look. 'Well, I wasn't expecting two boiled eggs for supper in the servant's hall!'

'My apologies. But Hugo's people from the colonies truly were deadly dull – you missed nothing.'

Daisy looks coquettish. 'I suppose it doesn't matter. Anyway, I had tea and cake and an interesting chat with the Queen.'

Kate drops the hairbrush. Fanny puts her hand over her mouth.

Fanny is wide-eyed with amazement. 'You did what?'

'I had tea with Queen Charlotte von Mecklenburg-Strelitz – the Queen of England. Mr Banks was there too.'

Fanny looks incredulous. 'Seriously? How on earth did that happen?'

'I bumped into her, and she invited me.'

Kate stands up, having recovered the hairbrush that had ended up under the bed. 'Excuse me, miss – what is she like?'

'Comely. And expecting a baby.'

Fanny sighs sympathetically. 'Yes, poor woman. That will be her eighth. At least I only have the two.'

Daisy looks at her. 'Two! You only have Esme.' Then, realising the implication, she rushes over to the bed to give Fanny a hug. 'That's what comes of being nice to your husband! But it's wonderful news.' She hugs her again.

Fanny breaks her sister's grasp, holds her at arm's-length and looks at her seriously. 'It is… providing I can give Hugo the heir he so desperately wants.'

The two share a moment's silence. Kate breaks the reverie.

'If you don't mind me asking, miss, what did you and the Queen talk about?'

Daisy mimes dipping a brush into water and painting a picture. 'She wants me to give her painting lessons.'

Fanny is even more amazed. 'My sister. Teaching the Queen to paint?'

'It is only to be an hour a day. Not too much distraction from my work for Mr Banks.'

'So, you mean to go to Kew every day?'

'Well, yes. I suppose, between Her Majesty and Mr

Banks, I must. Not Saturday nor Sunday, of course.'

'And who will be Esme's governess? And help me with the new baby?

'Oh, Fanny. That thought hadn't crossed my mind. I'm being so selfish. Look, I'll tell Mr Banks I cannot go.'

'Dear sister. I'm afraid you are now committed to a higher power than the mere Director of the Royal Gardens. Not to mention, this opportunity gives you exactly what you want from life – to be a painter, independent and valued.'

A MEETING OF MINDS

The following morning, Rupert is waiting for Daisy when her coach arrives through the gates and stops in the courtyard. He helps her alight, and they walk together towards the large greenhouse where the botanists work.

'Rupert, just how many specimens did Mr Banks bring back with him from his last trip?'

Rupert stops and looks pensive. 'I'm not sure of the exact number but over three thousand. And I cannot show you all of them, for much of what he brought back consisted of seeds accompanied by notes about the soil and the temperature and the moisture they require for successful propagation. But I can show you some of the plants themselves, if you'll accompany me to the hothouse.'

They walk on through the garden, Rupert exchanging nods and greetings with many of the gardeners at work.

Daisy is impressed. 'So many people, and you seem to know them all!'

Rupert grins. 'Most of them.'

'So how exactly do you come to be here, and what is it you do?'

'I'm a botanist. I study plants and their taxonomy – their families and how they reproduce and grow.' He rootles around in the pockets of his coat and brings out a bulb, a corm and a rhizome. 'For example, why does one flower grow from a corm, another grow from a bulb, and yet another grow from a rhizome? And how do they reproduce in comparison with flowers that set seed?'

Daisy looks awestruck. 'What a fascinating passion.'

'That's why I'm so lucky to have met Mr Banks at Cambridge where we enjoyed many captivating conversations. When he became Director at Kew, he knew my passion well enough to invite me to come and work with him.'

The pair stroll on a bit further with Daisy deep in thought.

'So, what does Mr Masson do then?'

'Well, he's a gardener. His fascination is the growing of plants and their husbandry – tending and caring for them.'

Daisy stops walking, turns to Rupert and looks at him. 'So, you look after the seeds, Mr Masson sows them in the ground and nurtures them, then somebody harvests the flowers so I can paint them?'

Rupert thinks for a moment. 'I've never thought of it that way, but yes, it is exactly that.'

'So, my paintings are the end result, the evidence that nature works.'

'Or more precisely, that nature worked once. Then I take the seed of that same new plant you have painted, give it to Mr Masson, and we try to prove that nature works in the same way again.'

'Then somebody harvests it, and we compare the result with my painting to see if it has reproduced truly?'

'And if it hasn't, we get very excited and ask why!'

The pair grin at each other. 'So, in a nutshell, Mr Fitzgerald, that is science!'

Rupert grabs the lapels of his coat and looks didactically down his nose at her. 'Technically, nuts are fruit.'

Daisy puts her hands on her hips. 'But, *sir*, I have to inform you that most nuts are also seeds.'

'But not all seeds are nuts.'

'And therein, sir, lies the logical, or perhaps illogical, conundrum.'

Looking rather pleased with themselves, they nod in agreement then stroll on some more, until Daisy touches his arm and stops him.

'I think then, for the purposes of science, I should paint the bulbs and corms and rhizomes and seed cases – or nuts, even – to show nature's journey from start to finish.'

Rupert purses his lips. 'What an extremely scientific and cyclical idea.' He hands Daisy the bulb, corm and rhizome he was showing her. 'Your first three specimens.'

Daisy drops him a curtsey and puts them in her apron pocket 'Thank you kindly, sir. What are they?'

'How on earth should I know? That's the fun of it! Until Mr Masson grows them, nobody knows.'

They walk on to the hothouse. Rupert indicates for Daisy to open the door and go in. As she enters, she catches her breath at the vista of hundreds of wonderfully exotic plants that meet her eye. Banks is working in his shirtsleeves. He looks up, smiles and beckons her in. Daisy walks over to him, followed by Rupert.

Banks makes an expansive gesture that embraces his domain. 'What do you think, Miss Salter?'

'Sir, this is truly magnificent.' She does a turn, taking in the panorama of floribunda stretching away on all sides, and she gives a deep sigh. 'There are so many strange and beautiful things. Do you expect me to paint all of them?'

Banks senses her nervousness. 'That is indeed the hope, Miss Salter. But one thing nature has taught me is that there is rarely a hurry – all things come to pass in their own good time.'

'Then, sir, I shall try. Or at least, I shall make a start, for who knows when I might finish?'

Banks rubs his hands together rather gleefully. 'That, Miss Salter, is exactly the attitude we scientists need. Start with a question and see what unfolds as the journey progresses.'

Straightening her shoulders, Daisy stands tall. 'More than attitude, I think I'll need a good degree of fortitude too.' Both men chuckle. 'Especially in this heat – I do not think I will be able to paint here, the humidity alone will play havoc with my pigments and paper.'

Banks frowns. 'Hmm, the chemistry and physics of the painting process is something I had not considered. What do you think, Rupert?'

'Well, I'm sure that if we take specimens to Daisy's studio'—Banks raises an eyebrow at Rupert's familiar use of Daisy's name—'for a few hours at a time, they will come to no harm.'

'I suspect you're right. As scientists, we have to

experiment.' He turns to Daisy. 'Now, *Miss Salter*'—he emphasises the polite address and looks admonishingly at Rupert—'what do you know about bulbs?'

Daisy rummages in her apron and pulls out the rhizome. 'That's not one, it's a rhizome.' She rummages again and pulls out a corm. 'Nor is that, that's a corm. Now, I know I have one somewhere...'

Daisy hands the corm to Rupert; he and Banks look amused. Daisy rummages some more, pulls out the bulb and holds it up to Banks. 'I knew I had one somewhere. There, Mr Banks, I do believe that is a bulb.'

Banks nods in agreement. 'And I do believe you are right, Miss Salter. But I have a man coming to meet me at eleven who wants to give me a thousand bulbs. Tulips, no less!'

Rupert looks at him with surprise. 'That's a gift fit for a king.'

Banks takes out a pocket-watch and checks the time. 'That is exactly what it is. If you could make the time to come and join us, Miss Salter, I feel your eye for colour will be an asset to our discussion.'

Daisy nods her assent. 'One thing, sir, would you mind if I asked you to call me by my christened name? We are not in my sister's salon making genteel conversation; we are making exciting discoveries together. Besides, being called Miss Salter makes me feel like an old maid.'

She looks him in the eye in a slightly challenging manner and holds his gaze, waiting for his response.

He purses his lips in thought. 'I suppose Daisy is an apt name for a flower painter – although as you are an

English Daisy, we should more properly refer to you as *Bellis perennis.*'

Rupert chimes in. 'Better that than *Leucanthemum vulgare.*'

Daisy looks at each of them in turn. 'Thank you for that consideration, gentlemen, but my family name is not *Asteraceae.* I am just a common or garden Daisy.' Feeling she has got the better of the exchange, or at least that the exchange has not got the better of her, she bobs a curtsey, turns and walks to the door.

Watching her go, Banks speaks aside to Rupert. 'Now that is something I very much doubt.'

TULIPS

A few minutes before eleven, whilst Daisy is closely considering a particular colour green in her studio, and Joseph Banks is reading a letter at his desk, a coach pulls through the gates, and a tall, well-built man gets out. He has long, blond hair tied in a ponytail and a leather satchel over his shoulder. He asks directions of a gardener and marches off along a path.

Daisy hears the courtyard clock strike eleven, comes out of her reverie, jumps up, reaches for her hat and pulls it on as she rushes out of the door. Fairly running towards Banks' office, she turns the corner of the building and collides with the man who has just arrived. She bounces off him, knocking his satchel off his shoulder in the process.

The man puts his hands out, catches her by her shoulders and holds her at arms-length, until she catches her breath.

Daisy brushes her hair back and puts her hat back on her head. 'I'm so sorry for barging into you.'

Van der Humm picks up his satchel. 'No damage done.'

The pair brush themselves down and take stock of

each other, recognition dawning. Daisy is first to speak, noting the way he is dressed.

'Meinheer, you look somewhat different than last time we met.'

Van der Humm straightens his lapels. 'When a Dutchman has an appointment to meet the Royal Gardener, a Dutchman dresses the part.'

Daisy nods appreciatively then, looking down, notices a couple of bulbs have fallen out of the satchel onto the path. She picks them up and offers them to him. 'Ah, you must be Mr Banks' tulip man?'

'Yes – I suppose, today, I *am* the tulip man.'

'Well, we had better not keep Mr Banks waiting. His office is through here. He has asked me to join you.'

With Van der Humm looking slightly mystified, Daisy opens the door and beckons him to follow her to Banks' office where she knocks and, upon being summoned to enter, goes in.

Banks has an extensive office: shelves lined with learned books, specimens in glass cases, candelabra, mirrors, an astrolabe and sundry bits and pieces of scientific equipment. He stands up from his long worktable and looks enquiringly at Daisy.

Daisy coughs politely. 'I'm sorry I'm late, Mr Banks, but I have found your tulip man.'

'My tulip man? Well come, meinheer. I see you have met Miss Daisy Salter.'

Van der Humm shakes Banks' hand. 'Yes, we bumped into each other outside.'

Banks looks slightly bemused. 'Well, excellent. Miss

Salter is our new "Painter in Residence". I've asked her to join us whilst we talk about our project. She has an excellent eye for colour.'

Daisy curtseys to him. 'Meinheer.'

The Dutchman bows. 'Miss Salter, I wondered if our paths might cross again, but I did not imagine it would be in circumstances such as these.'

All this time, Banks has been looking on, wondering what it is that he is missing.

'Meinheer did me the great kindness of rescuing my paints from a thief who had stolen one of my bags whilst I was changing coaches at the Barbican,' Daisy explains.

Banks looks between the two. 'Then he has already done one great favour for Kew. And I fervently hope he is here today to do a second.' Banks gestures to chairs set around the table and everybody sits. 'So, meinheer. What is your proposal?'

Van der Humm opens his satchel, and tulip bulbs spill across the table. 'Mr Banks, the Dutch government, which, as you will be aware, is in a state of flux due to what is happening in the American colonies, would like to gift its friend, England, a thousand tulip bulbs to plant in King George's gardens. I am instructed to offer my services to advise on the planting.'

Banks picks up a bulb and examines it closely. 'That is very generous, meinheer. On behalf of His Majesty King George, and Kew Gardens, I accept.'

'And you will assure His Majesty that Holland hopes the problems that face us both in the colonies will be resolved to our mutual satisfaction?'

'I will.'

The two men bow their heads in accord. Daisy looks on, becoming aware that this gift is about more than horticulture.

'The big question now is how and where we shall plant them,' Banks muses. 'Tell me some more about the bulbs you propose to gift.'

'Mr Banks, we plan to gift a mixture of tulips of different shades. In Holland, we plant them in straight lines to give impressive blocks of colour.'

Banks looks across to Daisy. 'Miss Salter, what do you think?'

Daisy takes a moment to consider. 'Well, sir, Mother Nature very seldom lumps plants of the same colour together in geometrical boxes. I think that blocks of colour would just look… well, like blocks of colour.'

Van der Humm juggles a couple of bulbs in his hands. 'So, what do you suggest?'

'If it was me, meinheer, I'd stand on the edge of the place they are to be planted, mix them up, throw them over my shoulder, let them land where Mother Nature intends and plant them as they fall.'

Banks looks enquiringly at Van der Humm. 'What say you, meinheer?'

The Dutchman puts the bulbs back on the table. 'Well sir, we Dutch like to be organised. We are a neat and tidy nation. We like structure. But that is not to say that we do not appreciate artistic inspiration. My country has produced some of the best artists in the world.'

Banks puts the palms of his hands flat on the table.

'Well, that is good news. Perhaps you and Miss Salter could find time to work together and come up with some sort of planting plan that will satisfy national and international niceties?'

Banks gives a no-nonsense look to both.

Van der Humm nods in acquiescence. 'Miss Salter, it would be a pleasure to work with you.' He tilts his head and gives her a wide smile.

Daisy is surprised to realise that she is blushing slightly and quickly lowers her eyes from his. 'Likewise, meinheer.'

Banks stands to signal that the meeting has ended. 'Meinheer, it is Friday today. Perhaps you can come and find Miss Salter on Monday?'

The tall, blond figure stands too. 'I would be delighted, Mr Banks.'

At the end of the day, as Daisy is walking back towards her waiting carriage, Rupert intercepts her and falls into step.

'So what was he like, your tulip man?'

'Very nice, but he does seem to be rather single-minded about the tulip.'

'Gardeners and botanists are passionate people – perhaps quietly passionate, but deeply passionate, nonetheless.'

'Yes. But at the same time there seemed to be more about the conversation than tulips.'

Rupert is quiet for a moment, considering his reply. 'The fact is, Daisy, that any gift of this sort is given with

political purpose'—Daisy raises her eyebrows in surprise—
'and often, these gestures are made between persons who
do not directly wield power but are close to those who do.
It's all rather clandestine.'

'Clandestine – now there's a thought or four.' Rupert
hands her up to the carriage. Daisy shuts the door and
is about to signal the driver to leave when she opens
the window. 'I don't suppose you know anything about
melons, by any chance?'

Rupert looks slightly smug. 'Quite a lot as it happens.
They're members of the Cucurbit family—'

Daisy looks at him indulgently. 'Ah, cucumbers and
gourds then.'

Rupert completely misses the irony in her tone.
'Exactly. However, when grown in captivity, so to speak,
they don't always self-pollinate that well and need to be
pollinated by hand.'

Daisy looks pensive. 'That's what I thought. We shall
see...'

Rupert is not quite following the plot. 'See what?'

'I've been helping Gardner with his melons.'

'Which gardener?'

'Gardner – my sister's gardener.'

'You've rather lost me, but if I can be of any help—'

Daisy reaches out and touches his arm. 'That's given
me an idea. If you are not busy on Sunday, perhaps you
could visit us in our greenhouse after church?'

'It would be a pleasure. Which church do you worship
at?'

'St Mary Magdalene, by Richmond Green.'

'Then I have an idea. Would your family mind if I joined you for the service?'

Daisy takes a moment to consider. 'I do believe we are all one in the eyes of God, Mr Fitzgerald. You would be most welcome.'

OF THE MAGDALENE
AND MELONS

The sun shines bright that Sunday morning and a peal of bells ripples through the air as Daisy and Fanny stroll arm-in-arm towards the church whilst Hugo strides ahead, bending the ear of a neighbour. Both women are dressed sensibly, bonnets tied demurely under their chins, Fanny nodding greetings to the ladies of the parish.

'Sister,' Daisy enquires, 'do you remember Mr Fitzgerald who attended the ball with Mr Banks?'

'The younger gentleman with red hair and freckles?' Daisy nods, and Fanny looks at her keenly. 'Has he expressed an interest in you?'

Daisy looks nonplussed. 'Certainly not. I've only known him but two days.'

Fanny gives her an old-fashioned look. 'Twenty-four hours can be plenty.'

Daisy raises her eyes to the heavens. 'Enough, sister! He's going to join us for the service and then I've invited him back to visit the greenhouse to see if he can apply his knowledge to help Gardner with the melons.'

Still looking slyly sideways, Fanny replies, 'I'm sure

that would be fine – Hugo complains bitterly that all the melon plants he has had sent from the colonies have proven to be a fruitless experiment – in every sense of the word.'

Rupert is waiting by the Lych Gate to greet Daisy. He bows and exchanges pleasantries with Fanny, and the trio enter the church.

After the service, Rupert and Daisy walk down the aisle behind Hugo and Fanny. They walk into the churchyard and pause, enjoying the sunshine, and Daisy introduces Rupert to Hugo.

'Brother, you remember Mr Fitzgerald?'

Hugo delivers his Sunday-best scowl. 'Yes, indeed, one of the men who has taken you away from looking after your sister and your niece.'

Rupert bows politely and says nothing.

Daisy continues. 'He has come from Kew specially to lend Gardner his wisdom.'

Hugo's scowl deepens. 'With those blasted melons? Might at least be some use then.'

Fanny squeezes Hugo's arm as if to calm him. 'Will you join us for luncheon, Mr Fitzgerald?'

'That's very kind, Lady Godolphin, but I am promised to join my parents for lunch in Kew.'

Hugo looks him squarely in the eye. 'Are they gardeners?'

Rupert refuses to rise to the implied insult. 'They have a house nearby, Sir Hugo.'

Hugo doesn't want to let it go that easily. 'And does your father work, sir?'

Rupert smiles amicably. 'He has a role with the Government, sir, that nobody apart from him seems to understand.'

Hugo harrumphs. 'Well, that's hardly unusual!'

Fanny is equally inquisitive. 'And does your mother keep a big house?'

'Lady Godolphin, my mother waits upon the Queen, in her retinue.'

Fanny smiles politely and, as Daisy and Rupert walk off down the church path chatting, Daisy's long hair swinging from side to side in time with her stride, Fanny holds Hugo back.

'Well, husband, he seems a very nice young man. From a family with royal connections.'

Hugo looks at her with disdain. 'Never trusted red-haired people myself. Anyway, for all you know, his father is a clerk and his mother a seamstress. Don't turn your matchmaking in that direction – she can do better. In fact, in her penniless state, she'll *have* to do better.'

In the gardens, Rupert and Daisy enter a hothouse where Gardner is busy. He looks up as the pair enter.

'Good morning, Mr Gardner. I'd like you to meet Mr Fitzgerald. He is a botanist from Kew Gardens, working with Mr Banks.'

Rupert is enthusiastic. 'I have been admiring your garden and your planting, Mr Gardner.'

Gardner smiles a slow smile. 'It is nothing to compare with the gardens at Kew, sir. Sometimes, on a holiday, I walk to Kew just to marvel at the planting. And the hothouses – such magnificence.'

Rupert inspects the plants on the greenhouse staging. 'I hear you're a melon man?'

Gardner looks at Rupert wryly. 'There's the question, sir. My master, Sir Hugo, is very fond of melons. In the colonies, my father had the knack of growing them, so it's become my personal challenge. Sir Hugo has the notion that we black men should have a natural affinity for melons.' He looks philosophically at his plants. 'I can grow most things, sir, but melons don't come quite so easily to hand. I get plenty of vine, but little fruit.'

Rupert inspects the vine, looking closely at the buds. 'You have fruit coming here, Mr Gardner. These flowers seem to have pollinated.'

Gardener peers in excitedly. 'I believe you are right, sir. Finally!' He looks round and beams at Daisy. 'That would be thanks to Miss Salter and her paintbrush.'

Rupert raises his eyebrows. Daisy gives a deprecating shrug.

'Well, Mr Gardner, Miss Salter, I will look forward to seeing the fruits of your endeavours!'

Rupert strides away to join his parents whilst Daisy returns to the house pondering what colours she would use from her palette to capture the copper lights in Rupert's hair.

'I think Mr Fitzgerald seems very eligible,' Fanny confides to Daisy that evening. 'And if he was at Cambridge University with Mr Banks, he must have a private income – or his family does.'

They are sitting in Daisy's bedroom, as they have become accustomed to do most nights, talking whilst Kate brushes Daisy's hair in front of the mirror.

'Do try to stop marrying me off, sister. Now I am painting at Kew, I will have plenty enough to occupy me. The last thing I need is a husband. And I shall be receiving my own private income soon.'

Fanny scowls. 'Take care to keep that quiet, Daisy, or Hugo will try and get his hands on your earnings. He's already muttering about how much it costs to have you living here and you no longer contributing.'

Daisy stops Kate brushing and turns around on her stool to face Fanny. 'Tell me, Fanny, why on earth did you marry that man?'

'You look like you've got a bad smell under your nose,' Fanny retorts.

Daisy stares at Fanny, shaking her head slightly from side to side. 'Well, why did you?'

Fanny stands up and walks to the window. 'I didn't want to live out my life in Suffolk. I wanted more than a quiet, country life, so when I came to do my season in London, marrying a lord with a sensible fortune seemed like a sensible way out.'

'But he's nearly thirty years older than you!'

'Somehow, that made him seem safe. All the men of my age were rakes or reckless or fortune hunters – and

I didn't have a fortune. Hugo wasn't so bad when he was wooing me – he knew things I didn't and was quite playful. How does any girl know what the future will hold after she walks down the aisle?'

Daisy shrugs. 'That seems good enough reason not to do it.'

'Easier said than done. Once you announce things, you get carried away with it all.'

Daisy looks unconvinced.

'Anyway, I felt sorry for him after the death of his first wife.'

Daisy's jaw drops and her eyes widen in astonishment.

'Hugo was married before?'

'That's why he is so much older than me. It's all a bit confusing, but he married the daughter of a cousin of Queen Augusta… or something like that. She had been married herself, but her husband had died when his horse fell on top of him. She had a son with her first husband, but she never managed to carry a child for Hugo. Then she died of a fever on one of Hugo's estates in the colonies, and her son with her. Hugo grieved for her bitterly.'

Kate has a sudden coughing fit. Fanny gives her a stare.

'You said I looked like I had a bad smell under my nose – now I know why. If that doesn't all sound conveniently fishy, I don't know what does! And I suppose Hugo inherited the tragic lady's fortune?'

Fanny bridles. 'I don't know what you're getting at – but it is time that I said goodnight.'

As the bedroom door slams shut, Kate returns to Daisy's toilette.

'Are you sickening for something, Kate?'

'Not at all, miss.'

'I thought for a moment you had a nasty cough coming on.'

'I'm fine, miss.'

'You didn't seem surprised by Lady Fanny's announcement.'

'Not the announcement about Lord Hugo's previous wife, miss, for I was on Lord Hugo's estate at the time she and the boy vanished.'

'Vanished?'

'Yes, miss. Lord Hugo took them both on a trip into the country to visit some new lands he was thinking of purchasing. Three weeks later, he returned with just the overseer he had also taken along, saying his wife and her son had contracted swamp fever, and there had been nothing he could do to save them. In his grief, he had buried them where they died.'

'Did the manservant have nothing to add?'

'He couldn't, miss. Lord Hugo had had his tongue cut out several years earlier.'

Daisy gasps and involuntarily raises a hand to her mouth. 'What do *you* think happened?'

'Slaves don't think, miss. And slaves don't listen, and if they do, they don't hear. But a few days later, when Lord Hugo took ship for England, bringing me with him, I wouldn't say he was full of grief all those times he had me called to his cabin at all hours of the day and night.'

That night, not for the first time since she had come to Godolphin House, Daisy's sleep is full of troubled dreams.

THE TULIP FIELD

Daisy in her painting clothes, and Van der Humm at his suave, finest, walk together through the gardens and out to an empty piece of ground.

'Kew is still in its early years, although there is talk King George intends to join up Princess Augusta's gardens with his own grounds at Richmond Palace. That's why there remains all this open space,' Daisy explains.

They stop and stand on a rise, overlooking a low area framed either side by trees that rise away from the Thames towards the horizon.

'This is the place Mr Masson has in mind for the tulips, meinheer. A splash of colour just below that brow.'

Van der Humm surveys the vista. 'Yes, the hangers of trees either side will focus the eye nicely from this vantage point.'

'If a path were planned to wind through the avenue of trees and across the grass, one could get close to the flowers. Tell me, meinheer – do tulips have a scent?'

'Not a strong scent, not in the sense of a perfume that a lady like yourself might wear. They are more to look at than to be sniffed at.'

'I do not wear perfume, meinheer.'

'Why not?'

'Because I have none to wear. And with so much glorious nature around, I see it as artifice.'

'You have obviously never been to Amsterdam.'

'Amsterdam?'

'Stinks of fish. Ladies wear perfume or a nosegay to keep the smell away.'

'Meinheer, I'm sure London is no better.'

'Quite. Stinks of horse manure, like at the Barbican. Lucky we're planting the tulips out here, where they at least stand a chance.'

Daisy takes out a sketchpad and pencil, and starts drawing. 'If I draw the background and the lay of the land, I can make watercolour sketches to show how it might look.' Van der Humm looks over Daisy's shoulder as the drawing takes shape. 'You know, if there were a grand house on the horizon, my old tutor, Mr Gainsborough, would be in his element.'

'Gainsborough?'

'Yes, very good at painting people in the countryside with large houses behind them.'

'Do you like painting people?'

'No. I prefer flowers and plants.' She closes her sketchbook and turns to Van der Humm. 'For all their beauty, flowers and plants have no vanity.'

Van der Humm looks at her with amusement in his eyes but refuses to rise to the bait. 'If you are planning some artistic impressions of how the planting might look, I have brought a book of plates showing the various colours of the tulips that will make up our gift.'

'I'd love to see them. Shall we return to my studio?'

Back in the studio, Van der Humm stands behind Daisy as she turns the pages of his catalogue. 'Meinheer, these are truly magnificent.'

There is a knock on the door, and Daisy looks up to see Banks enter.

'Mr Banks – come and see. These are the tulips we can choose from.'

Banks crosses the room, takes the book and reviews the pages. 'Meinheer, the variety and splendour simply amaze me. How should we possibly choose?'

Van der Humm put his hands out towards Daisy. 'As ever, I think Miss Salter has the solution. She has suggested painting some watercolour sketches that show impressions of how the various combinations of shades might look when planted.

'It wouldn't be entirely naturalistic,' Daisy admits, 'but I thought it would be a good way to consider how the planting might look when finished.'

Banks looks delighted. 'Why not? An artist's impression! I like that thought. How soon would we need to decide, meinheer?'

'The sooner the better. The bulbs are still in the ground, but we will lift them in the next two or three weeks. I can leave this book as reference for Miss Salter. I have other business to conduct but will return in perhaps a week's time?'

Daisy takes the book back from Banks. 'I'd love to show this to the Queen.'

In the distance a clock strikes.

Daisy jumps up. 'Three o'clock! Time for Her Majesty's first lesson.' Daisy grabs brushes and paper and rushes out.

Later that evening, Daisy sits sketching in the garden at Godolphin House, trying to make the most of the light, when Fanny appears and walks over.

Fanny sits down next to Daisy on her bench. 'I saw your man, Gardner, just now.'

Daisy laughs, 'He's not *my* man.'

'Daisy, be wary of Hugo – he doesn't like you being too familiar with the staff.'

'They are not exactly staff, Fanny. Besides, apart from you, there is no one else here to be familiar with. You seem to like Kate?'

'Yes, I do not feel comfortable that they are slaves.'

'I was reading in *The Gazette* that a young politician called Wilberforce plans to introduce a bill to ban slavery.'

'Hugo won't like that.'

Daisy gives Fanny a coy look. 'Not surprisingly, sister, I have no plans to tell him.'

UNEXPECTED GIFTS

The greenhouses at Kew Gardens are exactly that – the metal is painted a deep green and they are glazed with green-tinted glass. Daisy has happily fallen into an easy routine of collecting her specimens to be painted each day and setting them up in the studio before they are returned to their natural conditions each evening.

She is surprised one afternoon when there is a knock on the door and Van der Humm enters, hands behind his back. Daisy is equally as surprised to discover she is pleased to see him. 'Meinheer, I wasn't expecting you until next week.'

'I have taken a house just across the river in Brentford for the next few months. It is ideally situated in order that my tulip bulbs can be safely packed in straw and sent up the Thames with the tide to my wharf.'

'Do you cross by bridge or take one of the ferrymen?'

'The ferry is closer to my house.'

'And this means you will be close by to oversee the planting.'

'Yes. I am excited about that. But the reason I have come today is to bring a gift.'

'A gift? I don't get many gifts.'

Van der Humm takes his hands from behind his back and presents Daisy with an elegantly wrapped package tied with a bow. She looks at it, looks at Van der Humm and puts it on her bench.

Van der Humm looks on as she regards it. 'Well, open it.'

Daisy undoes the bow and unwraps the paper. Inside is a box printed with the word 'Floris'. Daisy opens the box.

Van der Humm leans towards her and whispers. 'Every lady should have perfume.'

Daisy opens the small bottle and waves it under her nose, then she closes her eyes and breathes in deeply. 'That, meinheer, is very heady.'

'It is what parfumiers call Orris – it comes from the corms of iris flowers. Or, more recently, from Jermyn Street in St. James's.'

'It is luxurious. Thank you so much.' She puts the stopper back in the bottle and the bottle back in the box.

'Will you not wear some?'

'I do not think it is for everyday use. Today, I will simply smell of Daisy.' She gives him a lovely smile.

'Perhaps, one day, you will have reason to wear some, when we are… together.'

Daisy smiles again. 'That would be… nice.'

Van der Humm bows, turns gracefully and leaves. The moment the door closes, Daisy reopens the box, opens the bottle, dabs a little perfume on her throat and breathes in deeply.

There is a second knock on the door, and Rupert

enters, smiling, with his hands behind his back. He sniffs the air, then goes across to the bench and sniffs various flowers. Looking mystified, he shrugs and turns to Daisy. I have brought you a gift.

'It is truly my lucky day, Mr Fitzgerald!'

Rupert raises an enquiring eyebrow then, as Daisy offers no more, he takes a package from behind his back. It is rather coarsely wrapped in brown paper and tied with string. He gives it to Daisy who looks at the package, looks at Rupert and puts it on her bench.

'Will you not open it? I am told it is something you have been asking for.'

Daisy unwraps it and extracts a metal object. 'You have brought me a caliper! Thank you.'

Rupert blushes. Daisy gets up, crosses to the bench, brushing past Rupert as she starts applying the caliper to making careful measurements of a wide leaf. 'Now I can be precise in the dimensions of my paintings. It is most useful. How did you come by it?'

'My father had it. He used to be in the Artillery and used it for measuring shot and ordnance.' Rupert sniffs again. 'What is that scent?'

'It is Orris, a perfume. Meinheer Van der Humm called in to see me just before you. He made a gift of it to me.'

Rupert's demeanour alters. He flushes with embarrassment and mutters grumpily, 'And I gave you a lump of old metal.'

Daisy reaches out and touches his arm. 'Dear boy, I shall use *your* gift every day.'

Rupert is not consoled. He turns on his heel, scowling.

Later that afternoon, Daisy is standing behind the Queen, examining the painting of two melons on a plate that the Queen is working on.

'Your Majesty, that is so lifelike you can almost smell them.'

'I do hope so. The King is very fond of sticking his nose into a pair of cantaloupes.'

The door opens and a servant enters bearing a tray of tea, closely followed by Banks.

'Mr Banks, what say you to the Queen's melons?'

Banks walks round and looks at the work. 'Very fine, Your Majesty. If Miss Salter ever breaks her painting arm, I shall know who to turn to!' Banks and Daisy sit down, and the Queen pours tea.

She passes a cup to Banks. 'Tell me, Joseph, during your three-year journey to the southern continents were you able to maintain standards and take tea at four?'

'When I could, Your Majesty. Although, if I can be so bold as to venture, you are not the only queen with whom I have taken afternoon tea. Indeed, I may be the only man in the world to have taken tea with a queen in both hemispheres.'

Banks looks slightly smug. Both women regard him with amazement.

The Queen speaks first. 'Pray tell, who was the other?'

'The Queen of Tahiti, Your Majesty. Where we stopped for several months to observe the transit of Venus.'

Daisy butts in, speaking excitedly. 'Was that the transit of June third in the year of sixty-nine?'

Now it is the turn of Banks to join the Queen in a look of amazement.

'Indeed, it was – you *are* well-informed.' Banks regards her curiously.

'I watched it with my father in his laboratory. We had a clear day in Suffolk with a light wind to blow the haze away. My father pointed his telescope to the sun, and we projected the image onto a piece of paper.'

The Queen smiles delightedly. Banks is quite flabbergasted.

'Well, Your Majesty, it seems that I might as well not have sailed the seven seas for three years.'

Daisy gushes on. 'Oh no, Mr Banks – if you had stayed here, you and Captain Cook would not have discovered the Australias.'

'I see you are *extremely* well-informed,' the Queen acknowledges.

'I try to be, Ma'am. My father always said that "an investment in knowledge pays the most interest".' The Queen and Banks study her in silence. 'Although he was quoting Mr Benjamin Franklin – who is American.'

Daisy looks worriedly towards the Queen who smiles fondly.

'Don't worry, my dear – I won't tell the King about your insurrectionist leanings. He already worries enough about the Americas.'

'Thank you, Ma'am.' Daisy makes her obeisance and leaves.

Banks sniffs the air. 'Your Majesty, there seems to be a distinct scent of irises in your room.'

'If I am not mistaken, Mr Banks, that is a perfume called Orris, from the Floris emporium in St. James's.'

'It is pleasantly floral, Your Majesty.'

'I like it very much. But I am not the one wearing it. It was young Daisy.' She leans forwards conspiratorially. 'And, as I doubt she has ever been to Jermyn Street, I do believe she has acquired an admirer. One with a generous purse into the bargain.'

NEWS UPON NEWS

Daisy is using Rupert's caliper to measure the fine details of a flower, before transferring the measurement to the painting she is working on. It is painstaking work, and she is totally focused – the tip of her tongue peeping out between her pursed lips.

The door opens suddenly, and Rupert bursts in, obviously excited. When he sees how hard Daisy is concentrating, he stops sharply and waits until she looks up.

'I see my father's ex-ordnance contraption is being put to good use.'

'Indeed. I feel much more in control when I can be this exact. What brings you here in such a rush?'

'I wondered if you'd heard the news?'

'News? No. What news?'

'Mr Banks is to be made President of the Royal Society!'

'Yet he is not yet thirty! He must have beaten many more established candidates for the position?'

'Following his three-year voyage on *Endeavour* around the southern continents, he has become the most preeminent natural scientist in the land. He was the unanimous choice.'

'How exciting. Will there be a ceremony? Will you attend?'

'There certainly will be. And I almost certainly will *not* be there.'

'But you are one of his closest confidantes.'

'Well, I have other news – I have asked Francis Masson to take me with him on his forthcoming plant-hunting trip to the Cape Peninsula.' He looks at Daisy keenly to see how she takes the announcement.

Daisy shrugs, only mildly perturbed, and turns back to her painting. 'And what has he said?'

'He has said, yes. I am to go.'

Daisy meets the news with nonchalance. 'Well done, I suppose that's good news. Looking at Mr Banks' achievements, travel and adventure seem a certain way to establish a man's reputation in the world. Albeit, the same opportunity would not be available to a woman.'

Rupert looks nonplussed. 'Will you not miss me?'

'A bit, I suppose. You are good company and a good friend. Yet, I already have so many flowers to paint, and you will doubtless bring back even more!'

'It can be dangerous, you know – Mr Banks took a painter, Sidney Parkinson, with him on *Endeavour*, and the poor chap died of the flux off Cape Town on the return voyage.'

'Rupert, I'm sure you have the constitution of an ox. The voyage to the Cape is well travelled with many islands en route to replenish your food and water. Just take care what you eat.'

'Well, Daisy, thank you for that advice!' he says to her back. Feeling chastened, he leaves.

Daisy is in the midst of the nightly hair-brushing ritual when Fanny enters looking rather pleased with herself.

'Daisy, I come with news!'

Daisy turns around. 'It seems I am to be presented with more news today than *The Gazette* publishes in a month.'

Fanny looks perplexed but carries on. 'Hugo has a guest for dinner on Friday.'

'Hmph. So more boiled eggs for supper for me. I'll ask Gardner to tell the chickens to put in some extra effort.'

'No, no! No. Hugo has said that you are to join us. Now you are the Queen's painting tutor, he has decided your company is perfectly acceptable.'

'So, something good has come of my painting. I suppose a good dinner will not go amiss. Who is the guest of honour?'

'Hugo will not say, other than that he is a well-to-do man of around thirty with whom he is hoping to do business. And the best thing is – I have ascertained that he is single.'

'He probably has warts on his nose. Sister, I do not want a husband of any description, let alone a warty one.'

Fanny bursts into giggles. 'You wicked girl. Now, if he has, I shall stare at them all evening.'

'One thing, sister, I do not think I have a proper dress to wear.'

Fanny pats her tummy. 'My current dresses would be too large, but I think I have something that you could make look fit and proper.'

'Yes, propriety is something I am having to learn a lot about where your husband is concerned. I'll need Kate's help, though.'

'Well, she's more your maid than mine. And if she can "help" land you a suitor, you are more than welcome!'

MR BROWN

O nce again, Daisy is intercepted by Rupert as she walks towards her office in the early morning sun.

'Mr Banks has requested that I bring you to him by the river – he has somebody he would like you to meet.'

'Are you going to tell me who it is?'

'Not allowed to. It's a surprise.'

The pair stroll companionably through the gardens towards a group of four men. Two are Banks and Masson. As they get close, Daisy gasps and grabs Rupert's arm. 'It's Mr Brown, the landscape architect.'

'Yes, Capability Brown. How do you know him?'

'His fame precedes him everywhere, of course, but I actually did meet him once, two years ago at the house of my neighbour, Mr Gainsborough. He won't remember me, though.'

Rupert gives her a sideways look. 'Is there no end to your connections – or coincidences?'

Capability Brown is a weather-beaten man, in his mid-fifties and conservatively dressed. The fourth man is his son, Lance, a Jack the Lad sort, in his early twenties. Banks welcomes them into the group. 'Miss Salter, can

I introduce you to Mr Lancelot Brown and his son Lance.'

Daisy bobs a curtsey. 'Mr Brown.'

Brown bows and stares closely at her. 'Miss Salter – I do believe we have met before?'

'We have indeed met, sir, but just the once.'

Brown snaps his fingers. 'Yes, I remember. Thomas Gainsborough's house.' He smiles, pleased at his recall.

'He was asking your advice on how best to construct the ideal landscape painting. You were asking his advice on which way the sunlight should fall so your landscapes look their best.'

'And if I remember, you were painting flowers, which I greatly admired.' He turns to Banks. 'Well, Joseph, this is a coincidence. Then again, perhaps not, for I suppose I should not be surprised to find a painter of Miss Salter's botanical talent in the greatest garden in England.'

Banks beams proudly. 'I like to think we have the finest examples of everything at Kew, Lancelot. Including botanical experts.'

Brown nods and looks to Daisy. 'Well, Miss Salter, I look forward to seeing some more of your work.'

'Your wish shall be granted sooner than you might think, Lancelot. Miss Salter is working on another project here, painting "artist impressions" to show how the finished tableau might look.'

Brown regards Daisy with interest. 'Did Mr Gainsborough teach you about landscape painting too, Miss Salter?'

'A little, although I was never adept with oils. I mostly

use watercolours for my work. They are, as Mr Banks says, "impressions" not paintings.'

Masson speaks for the first time. 'Yet they are much better than relying on simple imagination. Mr Brown has accepted a commission to turn this dead piece of land into a new walkway.'

Brown warms to his subject. 'Yes, I plan to construct a "Hollow Walk". I have some sketches here.' He gestures to his son Lance who takes papers from a satchel and passes them to him. 'But I do believe some colour would make them more credible.'

Daisy looks at them and compares them to the landscape. 'Yes, I see. Yes. I like that. If I may be so bold, sirs, I would say this all looks extremely "capable".'

The men smile and laugh at Daisy's cleverness.

Masson, as ever, is the practical voice. 'Miss Salter, would these be comprehensive enough for you to prepare an "impression"?'

'Yes, but it would be of great assistance if Mr Brown could also give me a planting plan, if he has one? Then I could match the colours.' Daisy looks to Brown.

'Indeed, I have. Yet, it still needs a little work. Would it be possible for Lance to bring it to you in a few days' time?'

'I have no plans other than to be here in my studio. Oh, and to give Her Majesty her lesson.' She looks to Lance. 'Could you possibly come at two o'clock on Thursday?'

Lance nods. Then, when nobody is looking, and somewhat to her consternation, he winks at her.

Daisy and Rupert leave the men discussing the finer

details and stroll back together towards the main campus.

'If I may say so, Daisy, you have made your mark on Kew in a very few weeks. How do you find having men like Mr Banks and Mr Brown seek your counsel?'

Daisy considers. 'I can't say I've really thought about it. I think what I say is common sense. In my experience, most intelligent men respond well to that.'

'Daisy, you are a lady with very honest and refreshing views on the world.'

'When viewed honestly, Rupert, I have always found the world to be a rather refreshing place.'

BLACK TULIPS

Downstairs, the dining table has been laid with silver and crystal, and the candelabra lit in preparation for Hugo's guest. Upstairs, Kate is dressing Daisy for dinner. Her gown is understated, a soft green, complementing the auburn highlights in her hair. She looks elegant and womanly, her confidence growing daily.

Kate admires the finished creation whilst she fusses round the hem of the gown. 'You look beautiful, miss.'

'Thanks to you, Kate.'

Kate takes the compliment in her stride. 'I understand there is an unmarried gentleman attending this evening.'

'Kate, unmarried men have little interest for me and, in my experience, even less interest in me.'

'Looking like that, miss, a single man would be mad not to be interested.'

'If I were ever to marry, I would prefer a man who was interested in me for who and what I am, rather than how I look. Looks, like flowers, fade. Yet over the years, and with maturity, gardens grow more interesting.'

'You are an intelligent and talented woman. Why has no man ever snapped you up and made you his wife?'

'None have ever asked me.'

'Surely, there must have been *one*?'

'None in my past.'

'And in your present?'

'None that have ever asked me.'

'What if you were to be asked in the future?'

'Then I would carefully consider my answer... which would almost certainly be no.'

Daisy stands up and swishes her dress in front of the mirror. 'Now, Kate, pass me that box from Floris. Just in case the man who might make me change my mind is in the drawing room, I may as well smell my best.'

Kate passes Daisy her perfume. She dabs it on her wrists and throat.

Hugo, Fanny and Daisy are sitting drinking wine when a black footman enters. 'Lord Hugo, Meinheer Van der Humm.'

The ladies stand, and Van der Humm, looking extremely dashing, enters smiling. Hugo welcomes him. Daisy looks surprised.

Hugo is at his personable best. 'Meinheer Van der Humm – may I introduce my wife Lady Godolphin.' Fanny curtseys and Van der Humm bows. 'And my wife's sister, Miss Daisy Salter.'

Van der Humm bows low over her hand and breathes the scent from her wrist. 'Miss Salter, may I say that is a very elegant perfume you are wearing.'

Daisy curtseys. 'Thank you, sir. It is Orris. What a

pleasant surprise to see you here.'

Hugo and Fanny have been looking on, bemused by the subtle flirting. 'A surprise?' Hugo asks. 'Have you met before?'

Daisy nods. 'Several times. Meinheer Van der Humm has a project with Mr Banks at Kew, a project with which I have some involvement.'

'Actually, Lord Hugo, Miss Salter is responsible for bringing the project to life, not to mention changing the opinions of men who perhaps need some impetus to their thinking!'

A servant announces that dinner is served, and the quartet move to the dining room where Daisy sits across the table from the Dutchman, the two exchanging surreptitious glances. He is witty with a baritone voice, which the accent makes exotic. The conversation is pleasant, and even Hugo seems in good humour. As the meal comes to a conclusion, Fanny puts down her glass and stands. The men stand in unison.

Fanny is, as ever, the gracious hostess. 'Meinheer, it has been a pleasure to have such excellent and entertaining company this evening. We ladies will retire and leave you to your port wine, and your business conversation.'

Daisy stands too. 'Will you be talking about tulips?'

Van der Humm's eyes twinkle. 'Tulips. Yes, indeed. Your brother and I have a plan to grow and import rare black tulips.'

Hugo, in the midst of a swig of wine, coughs and almost chokes.

'Are you all right, husband?'

Hugo coughs into his handkerchief. 'I'm fine. My wine went down the wrong way.'

'Well, providing you are all right, we'll leave you to your conversation.' Fanny and Daisy leave. Hugo signals for port to be poured and dismisses the servant.

'Black tulips – that's a fine conceit, meinheer!'

'Given the crop you are growing in the colonies, it seemed rather appropriate.'

Hugo smirks as Van der Humm continues. 'You have a reputation, Sir Hugo, for importing fine quality flowers ripe for pollinating. My associates have a ready market in Holland for such a cargo.'

'You are not mistaken, sir. The lines established by my father are from the best African rootstock and have been selectively bred by my family for decades, often with the inclusion of some noble white blood.'

Van der Humm nods approvingly. 'My principals in this business would be most interested in coming to an accommodation with you for a regular supply. Naturally, I would need to… examine the merchandise.'

'As luck would have it, I have a cargo arriving in Liverpool in a few days' time. I will be meeting it personally. Why don't you come with me? You would have the opportunity to pick and pluck the flower of your choice.'

Van der Humm stands, drains his port and makes a small bow. 'That is an interesting proposition. But Liverpool? You do not bring your cargo in through Bristol?'

'I used to. But there is a Member of Parliament,

Wilberforce, who has men active in the area trying to stamp out the black tulip trade. I prefer to keep things, shall we say, clandestine.'

In the drawing room next door, still in their finery, Fanny and Daisy are sitting talking.

'I must say your Dutch friend is very easy on the eye. And I have never seen you so charming – or trying to be.' She raises her chin, challenging for a reply.

Daisy doesn't rise to the bait. 'If you say so, sister.'

Fanny has no intention of letting it go. 'It was him who gave you the perfume, was it not?'

Daisy blushes and giggles. 'How did you guess?'

'The way your eyes sparkled when you spoke of it. 'Don't you find him handsome, Daisy?'

'He is manly, like Papa was manly. He seems a reliable horticulturalist.'

'Yes, one would expect a Dutch flower merchant to be reliable. Although I'm not sure I'd expect a man described so to be very exciting. Anyway, I'll ask Hugo to find out more about him and his prospects.'

'Oh, sister, do you have to matchmake for me?'

'Somebody does. And it will at least make Hugo think we're trying.'

The door opens, and the two men enter. Hugo is still smirking. 'Meinheer is about to leave, but we both travel to Liverpool together next week to examine a cargo.'

Daisy looks excited. 'Black tulips? I would love to see one.'

Van der Humm has moved to Daisy's chair and puts one hand on her shoulder. 'We're hopeful, but they have to be planted in the spring, and then we'll see how they bloom. It is an uncertain science.'

Fanny's eagle eye has not missed the hand on the shoulder. 'How nice. It will be good for you to have such pleasant company for your trip, husband.' As both men walk out of the door, she winks at Daisy. 'This is a business we must encourage, sister!'

THE BLACK PIG

Van der Humm has taken a house on the Thames for good reason. The river is both a major highway, with ferries and lighters crossing between banks, and barges carrying all manner of goods upstream from the Port of London, and a busy home to much nefarious business that makes use of the many small creeks running into the main flow. It offers hidden landing stages, dark and mysterious places ideal for dark deeds, and inevitably, a hideaway inn or two. On a night when the moon is new and the sky is black, it is at just such a place, the Black Pig, that Van der Humm alights from a small boat.

He tosses the boatman a coin and goes to the door. The windows are dimly lit with candles. He enters and looks around, then at the barman who nods and jerks his thumb towards a door at the back of the inn. Van der Humm walks across the bar and knocks on the door. A guttural voice responds.

'*Komen*!'

Van der Humm enters the room. A man with black hair and a black beard, both streaked with silver, dressed in black, his dark eyes vibrant behind wire-rimmed spectacles, is sitting alone by a fire, smoking a pipe. There is a table with two glasses and a stone bottle. The man beckons Van der Humm to the seat opposite and fills the glasses with a clear liquid.

'*Jenever. Hoe gaat het met je?*'

Van der Humm tastes his gin. '*Goed bedankt.*'

Their eyes meet and the older man regards him in silence for a moment. He sees that Van der Humm is not entirely comfortable.

'Meinheer de Vries, you sent for me.'

'Be easy, Johannes, I just want to know – what news can I report to our masters at The Hague?'

Van der Humm fidgets slightly in his chair 'Good news, meinheer.'

De Vries takes off his glasses and polishes them. 'Good news? Well, that is… good. But could you be more specific?'

Van der Humm makes an expansive inviting gesture.

'Don't play games with me Johannes, I have too much on you for that. What news of our slave business?'

'I go with that pompous man, Godolphin, to Liverpool to inspect a cargo.'

'Excellent! You will negotiate the delivery of a similar cargo to Rotterdam?'

Van der Humm nods and sips his drink.

'And will you mention tea to him?'

'Yes, he is a greedy man, and I have an idea that will both save him time and make him more money.'

'And how goes our project at Kew Gardens? Have you managed to ingratiate yourself with Banks?'

'Better, meinheer. I have negotiated the deal with

Banks, who is most grateful. The news is that he is soon to become President of the Royal Society and there are rumours of a knighthood.'

De Vries smiles appreciatively and nods.

'But there is more, meinheer.'

De Vries leans forwards in anticipation. 'More?'

'I have also ingratiated myself with a young woman who is Banks' protégé as a botanical "Painter in Residence".'

De Vries leans back dismissively. 'What benefit is a girl to our schemes?'

'She is Godolphin's wife's sister.'

'That may be convenient.'

Van der Humm sits up straight, enjoying having left the best until last. 'But there is more.' De Vries leans forwards again, all attention on Van der Humm. 'The girl, Daisy, has become Queen Charlotte's personal painting tutor.'

De Vries sips his gin and regards Van der Humm over his spectacles. Slowly, an ever–broadening grin crosses his face, and he chuckles.

'Yes, that *is* good news, Johannes. I will write to our masters and seek their guidance on how we can make the most of this opportunity. Presumably, I can reassure our masters that you are doing all you can to make yourself attractive to the girl?'

'Indeed, meinheer. She has talent as a painter but is a simple country girl from Suffolk. I think she will be... shall we say... accommodating.'

De Vries pulls a purse from his pocket and throws it to Van der Humm who deftly catches it and makes a small bow. 'If these things come to a satisfactory conclusion, and you beget yourself a daughter, you might like to call her Tulip. Anyway, when the time is right, I will give you more funds to buy something special for this Daisy girl. And I have a gift waiting for you in the chamber above – I think you have earned a little bonus.'

'Most kind, meinheer. A black tulip?'

De Vries takes off his glasses and regards Van der Humm with a mixture of amusement and contempt. 'Meinheer Van der Humm, we both know that black tulips are even more rare than unicorns. And the gift that awaits is no unicorn either. But she is a feisty chestnut filly who will doubtless prove an interesting ride.'

Van der Humm nods, turns and walks to the door. Just as he gets there, de Vries speaks.

'And Johannes?' Van der Humm stops and looks round. 'Try not to get bucked off.'

FIRST IMPRESSIONS

By now Daisy has had enough time with Van der Humm's illustrated tulip manual to prepare her artistic impressions of the tulip field. Daisy, Banks, Masson, Rupert and Van der Humm are standing round Daisy's workbench, studying them.

Banks takes the lead. 'It's not an easy choice. Six options are almost too many to choose between.'

The men look to Daisy for her response. 'Well, I don't know that any should be considered the finished article. I wanted to show the range of colour variations and densities of planting.'

Banks turns to Masson. 'Francis, you're the gardener here. What do you think?'

'I think I prefer the density of the planting to be greater closer to the path, fading away as the eye moves up the slope until it vanishes. Rupert?'

Rupert points to the sketch he prefers. 'I tend to agree. And I prefer the deeper colours being towards the outsides, framing the other colours. Meinheer?'

'It is very new thinking to me. But your landscape traditions, with the hills and slopes and falling water, are very different to our flat lands.'

Banks makes the diplomatic choice. 'I think I concur with Francis and Rupert – but I will show these to the Queen and ask her if she wants the King to decide. Meinheer, will you stay and take lunch with me?'

'I thank you for your invitation, sir, but I must join Miss Salter's brother now. We travel this afternoon to Liverpool, hopefully to inspect a cargo of black tulips.'

Ever the gardener, Masson, looks interested. 'Liverpool seems a strange place to land plants from Holland, meinheer?'

'Some of my Dutch friends have been experimenting with planting in the dark peat of Ireland. We will see the bulbs bloom next year.' He turns to Daisy and bows low. 'Miss Salter, thank you for your artistic endeavours. Your naturalistic creativity has caused scales to fall from my eyes.' Van der Humm and Daisy hold eye contact for long enough to be meaningful, which brings a frown to Rupert's brow. Van der Humm bows again and leaves.

Masson is perplexed. 'Black tulips, indeed! And from Ireland at that. Rupert – you have Irish family: have you heard of such a thing?'

Rupert is equally mystified. 'I have to say, Francis, that I have not. But I will make enquiries with my Irish connections.'

As the coach-and-four bearing Hugo and Van der Humm passes a milestone bearing the legend 'Liverpool 5', the conversation turns to the purpose of their visit.

'You are aware of the British interest in the "triangular trade", meinheer?'

The Dutchman nods. 'Indeed – whilst many of my countrymen tend to look to the East Indies for their fortune, some in my acquaintance run goods down to West Africa in exchange for slaves captured by rival tribes to transport to the Caribbean or the colonies in America. Then return with goods to sell to merchants in Amsterdam.'

Hugo looks slightly surprised. 'Didn't know you Dutch had that much of an interest?'

'It's a matter of history, Hugo. Don't forget, what you now call New York was originally New Amsterdam. And New Amsterdam was the capital of New Netherlands.' He looks sideways at his travelling companion. 'Until you English sent a fleet to capture it.'

Hugo sneers. 'Never been one for history. Rum's the big import for England, of course. That and tobacco.'

Van der Humm is all equanimity. 'We prefer gin ourselves. Although tobacco is a very fine thing.'

'I grow a lot of tobacco on my plantations. That and cotton further south.'

'Not to mention black tulips.'

'Best not to mention them where we can be overheard, if you please.' Hugo scowls. 'Don't want other people to know my business.'

The coach rattles along the Liverpool dockside through the damp, misty evening, stopping outside an inn typically called the Black Boy, the sign only just discernible in the light of torches burning outside. Hugo and Van der Humm get out. Bags are handed down, Hugo pays and dismisses the driver, and the pair enter the premises. An imposing man of mixed-race, in his mid-forties, his hair cropped and greying, better dressed than others in the inn, with a bit of a swagger about him and a riding crop under his armpit, is at the bar. He waves Hugo and Van der Humm over. The pair cross to meet him.

Hugo makes the introduction. 'Meinheer Van der Humm – this is Uriel, my plantation manager in Virginia.' Van de Humm and Uriel nod to one another. Uriel silently picks up a flagon and three pewter tankards and, with a gesture of his head, leads them to a nearby staircase. The three ascend and enter a room.

Inside is a table and three chairs. Across the room, six young black women sit manacled to more chairs, naked from the waist up. A white man sits in the corner looking over them. Uriel indicates that Hugo and Van der Humm should sit down. He puts the tankards on the table and fills them from the flagon.

Hugo lifts a questioning eyebrow at Van der Humm. 'First impressions, meinheer?'

Van der Humm runs his eyes over the women in discerning fashion. 'Excellent! Although I must say, Lord Hugo, your man doesn't say a lot.'

'I took his tongue out. Safer that way.'

Van der Humm's eyes widen, and he looks away. Hugo grins, his eyes hard and cruel, glad to learn that the normally implacable Dutchman can be shocked by some things. Uriel walks across to the manacled women and makes them stand up. When one refuses, he clips her across the shoulder with his stick.

'Take care not to spoil the merchandise; she is not yet sold,' Hugo cautions.

Uriel beckons Van der Humm to come closer to examine the girls. As he walks along the line-up, Uriel uses his stick to lift up a breast or part the skirt to show Van der Humm what is on offer.

Hugo observes the proceedings. 'Uriel – I hope none of these girls were touched during the crossing?' Uriel makes an affirmative gesture with his head.

'Well, meinheer, in that case you can choose your flower and pluck her in your chamber with no fear of the pox.'

Van der Humm is, as ever, well-mannered. 'Surely you should have first pick?'

'To be honest, meinheer, there is not really one to my taste.'

Van der Humm nods his acquiescence and walks down the line appraising the women before indicating the one of his choice. The white attendant gets up, frees her from the manacles and leads her off to a room at the side.

Hugo smiles and waves Van der Humm away. 'Enjoy, meinheer. She is typical of the merchandise I can supply. Don't worry for your safety, she will be shackled to the bed.'

Van der Humm pauses. 'Do you import young bucks too?'

Hugo stares at him blankly. 'What would be the point in that? Or... do you prefer boys? If so, I could arrange for that on the next trip.'

Realising just what Hugo's business is, Van der Humm

frowns. He shakes his head to the proposal, makes a polite bow and follows the route the girl took into the side room.

After the door closes, Hugo regards his manservant. 'As I said, Uriel, there is not *one* girl to my taste – I'll take *two* – that black one and the light-skinned girl. It's unlikely she's one of my by-blows from coupling during my visits, but no matter if she is.'

Uriel smiles, his mouth full of blackened teeth, and undoes the girls' manacles. Hugo puts some coins on the table. 'I know you prefer white flesh; there's plenty of that to be had in Liverpool port. Now cover these last three girls up and take care of them – we have buyers viewing them tomorrow.'

Both men are in fine form as they break their fast at the inn the following morning. Van der Humm is tucking into a pair of kippers. 'I'm obliged to you for last night, Lord Hugo. I think I may have a way of paying you back – with interest.'

Hugo talks around a mouthful of ham and eggs. 'No need, meinheer, it was a means to seal our business arrangement, with my compliments.'

'In fact, sir, it is a second business arrangement I have in mind. One that might greatly benefit us both.'

Hugo wipes his mouth with the back of his hand. 'I'm listening.'

'Let me ask you a question first. When might you expect the next cargo of the sort we inspected yesterday?'

'Difficult to be precise when it comes to the triangular

trade. Depends on the weather. I normally plan for five to six months. Although it can be quicker.'

'A cumbersome and risky trade then, and you are reliant on the slaves surviving the journey.' Van der Humm holds eye contact with Hugo.

'I'm still listening, meinheer.'

'What if I could employ your ships by filling them with a valuable cargo they could take directly to the Americas? You make money the moment you arrive, then you simply turn your ships around, filled with whatever goods you have to collect along with a complement of black tulips, and sail straight back to England.'

Hugo picks up his cup of coffee, all the time regarding Van der Humm over the rim of the cup. 'Enlighten me, meinheer. What cargo could I transport from here to the Americas and sell at a profit?'

'The cargo is not here, sir. It is in a warehouse on the Isle of Man.'

'But you have yet to tell me what it is.'

'Tea.'

'Tea? I was under the impression, meinheer, that the tea trade with the Americas was the province of the East India Company.'

'Mostly, you are right. But your government puts such a high tax on it that there will always be a market outside of official channels. We could either supply the tea and simply pay you for the transit to our own contacts, or you could find your own market.'

Van der Humm can sense the cogs whirring in Hugo's mind. 'How exactly is the tea packed, meinheer?'

'In the middle of sealed containers with tulip bulbs all around the outside so it passes examination. It is all quite clandestine.'

'Meinheer, I think we may be able to come to an accommodation – provided the financial aspects make sense.'

'Good, my lord – you will find my principals quite generous. There is only one proviso. On the first voyage, they would expect you to personally travel with the goods to ensure there are no… complications.'

'I have no problem with that, meinheer. I've been thinking of visiting my estates for a few months, especially as my wife is due to whelp me a new pup. In my experience, childbirth is no place for a man – he's better off out of it. I've no interest going to Manx, though. I'll send Uriel to collect the goods then they can call in and collect me in Bristol when they take on clean water.'

Van der Humm holds his hand out across the table. 'That is acceptable.' The two men shake hands.

RUTLAND

Having returned late, Hugo slept in his dressing room, so Fanny does not see him until he comes down to join her at breakfast. He enters the breakfast room, goes to the sideboard, helps himself to food and sits down.

'Husband, how were your black tulips?'

'More brown than black, but the Dutch prefer milk in their coffee, and Van der Humm seemed to like them well enough.'

'Did you and he do business together?'

'Yes, I am to ship an order he placed direct to Rotterdam.'

Daisy enters and goes to take breakfast. 'Good morning, brother, sister.'

Hugo ignores her and continues speaking to Fanny. 'I will oversee the business myself whilst I am in Virginia.'

Fanny drops her cutlery with a clatter and looks incredulous. 'Virginia! When?'

'I leave in ten days from Bristol. The conflict with the backwoodsmen in the Carolinas is spreading, and I need to oversee the securement of my property.'

Fanny looks aghast. 'But that is three months at sea

even in good conditions… and then you will need to spend time there before making the journey back!'

The reply is nonchalant. 'Yes, I expect to be away for more than half the year. What of it?'

Fanny's lip trembles, and she holds her napkin to her mouth. 'I'm having your baby!'

He looks at her growing belly. 'Yes, it hasn't escaped my notice. It will come, with or without my presence.' He stares pointedly at Daisy. 'You have your useless sister to provide any necessary help.'

Daisy quietly eats her breakfast with her head down.

Fanny is in full flow. 'You can't leave me here by myself!'

Hugo puts his knife and fork down with a bang. 'Which is why, *my dear*, I am shutting up this house and sending you to my brother Greville. There are perfectly good midwives in Rutland.'

Daisy suddenly looks up. 'Shutting the house? Where will I live?'

Hugo looks despairingly at her. 'Are you an idiot? You'll go to my brother's, of course, see your sister through her confinement and be governess to Esme. I've written to Greville and told him that by the time I get back he is to have found some country squire or parson to marry you and take you off my hands.'

He stands up, wipes his hands on a napkin, throws it onto the table and strides out. Daisy and Fanny look at each other in dismay.

'Oh dear, Greville is not a nice man.' Fanny wipes a tear from her eye.

'Greville is not a nice man! You mean he's worse than your husband?'

'Hugo isn't so bad.'

Daisy stands, walks around the table and hugs Fanny. 'I shall so miss Kew.'

'It would be a shame for two of us to be miserable in Rutland. I'll try and persuade Hugo to let you stay.'

'Well, I can't see that being "nice" to him is going to work this time.' Daisy hugs her tighter, wondering what on earth Banks will think and what the Queen will say.

It is a warm afternoon, and the windows are open in Queen Charlotte's parlour. There is a humming of bees, and the ripe fulfilment of summer is pregnant on the air. The Queen sits balancing a board between her gravid belly and her desk, painting. Daisy stands looking over her shoulder. A drop of water falls onto the paper.

The Queen is about to turn around to locate its source when there is a knock on the door and a woman enters. She is strikingly handsome, tall, red-haired and very elegantly dressed. Without hesitation, she walks across the room and curtsies deeply.

'Your Majesty.'

The Queen is slightly flustered. She puts her brush down, stands up, hesitates then goes to sit on the sofa. 'Daisy, I do not think you have met my great friend and chief lady-in-waiting, the Countess of Clonmel.'

Daisy wipes her eyes and curtsies.

'Her Majesty wrote to me about her lady-in-painting.

I must say you look more like a lady in tears?' Daisy starts crying again. The countess kindly takes her hand and leads her to a seat.

The Queen is equally comforting. 'My dear – whatever is the matter?'

'Ma'am, my brother Hugo is soon away to the colonies on business, and I am told I must move to Rutland, with my sister.'

'From your tears, can I assume that Rutland does not appeal?'

'In truth, Ma'am, I know nothing of Rutland.'

The Queen looks enquiringly at the countess for a comment. 'Few do, and probably best kept that way, Ma'am.' The Queen shrugs in agreement.

Daisy wipes her eyes. 'I just know I do not want to leave Kew. My work here makes me feel I have worth in my own right… and, of course, I will miss teaching Your Majesty.'

The Queen looks concerned. 'I dare say Mr Banks won't be very pleased to lose your talents either. He showed me and the King your impressions of Mr Brown's plans for his Hollow Walk. The King was most taken with them.'

Daisy is incredulous. 'The King has seen my paintings?'

'Well, I thought that was the whole point of you creating them. They were most convincing. I do believe His Majesty showed them to Lord Fox, the Prime Minister.'

Daisy's face lights up in surprise and delight. The two older women exchange glances.

'Well, my dear, off you trot – the countess has been

104

visiting her home in Ireland for the past few months, and we have much to say to each other.'

Daisy's ears prick up. 'Ireland? Did you see any black tulips?'

The countess looks perplexed. 'Black tulips? Not at all. Why ever do you ask that?'

'I was talking about it with Mr Banks, Mr Masson and Rupert, but Rupert didn't think there were any there.'

Daisy remembers where she is, puts her hand over her mouth, curtsies to both women and leaves.

The countess looks enquiringly at the Queen. 'Rupert? Ma'am?'

'It would seem that Daisy has formed a close friendship with your son. Although perhaps he is fonder of her than she of him, for the moment.' The countess raises an eyebrow. 'Anyway, Madeleine, we must see what we can do to keep Daisy at Kew.'

The countess is quick to reply. 'There is that empty cottage in the gardens behind the orangery, Ma'am.'

'Good idea, although undoubtedly full of spiders. Then again, Daisy claims to be a woman of science, so a few arachnids shouldn't bother her. I'll talk to Banks. In the meantime, you might like to visit her family in Richmond?'

A carriage emblazoned with the royal coat of arms sweeps through the gates at Godolphin House, and an elegant footman helps a tall woman step down from the compartment. Fanny and Hugo are sitting in their drawing room when the footman enters and presents Fanny with a calling card. Fanny reads the card and immediately rises, in rather cumbersome fashion, to her feet.

'Hugo! Stand! We have a visitor.'

Hugo stands, and the footman returns with the Countess of Clonmel. The footman bows. 'Lady Madeleine, Countess of Clonmel, Sir Hugo, your ladyship.' The footman backs out.

Hugo, knowing he is significantly outranked, bows obsequiously. Fanny makes a clumsy pregnant curtsey. 'Milady, won't you sit?'

'Thank you.' She sits. 'Sir Hugo, Lady Fanny, I have heard so much about you from your sister.'

Hugo looks nervous. Fanny looks stunned.

'You may know that I am Queen Charlotte's chief lady-in-waiting?'

Hugo and Fanny both nod.

Hugo finally finds his voice. 'To what do we owe the honour of this visit, milady?'

'The Queen, who shares your happily gravid state Lady Fanny, has asked me to come and see you with regard to her... lady-in-painting, Miss Salter.'

'Daisy? Is she all right?'

'She does very well. The Queen is rather taken with her teaching, and Mr Banks sings her praises on a daily basis. She does so well that the Queen would like her to come and live at Kew.'

'What? No. It is arranged that she is to go to the country and look after Lady Godolphin and our daughter whilst I am in the colonies.'

Fanny looks aghast at Hugo's bad manners.

'I'm afraid that won't be convenient for Her Majesty. But she has anticipated the impact of your loss and would like to offer one of her own governesses to accompany Lady Fanny and provide her with assistance. To be honest, having had so many children, the Queen has governesses to spare.'

Hugo and Fanny are dumbstruck.

The countess looks satisfied. 'Well then, that's settled,' She stands, and Hugo and Fanny stand too. 'Please sit, Lady Fanny. Tell me, when are you due?'

'October. It is my second.'

'If that is the case, I believe Her Majesty will deliver before you. This will be her eighth confinement, and her offspring tend to arrive as clockwork.'

The countess moves towards the door.

'Excuse me, milady, do *you* have children?'

The countess stops and turns around. 'Yes, I have been blessed three times – a girl, then a boy, then another girl.'

'I hope for a boy, milady, this time.'

The countess looks sympathetic. 'All women do. I wish you luck. Oh, Miss Salter will be needing suitable clothing for the evenings, and a maid.'

'We will see to that, milady.'

Hugo stands in the shadows, looking disgruntled, furious that he has been outmanoeuvred.

THE COTTAGE

Meanwhile at Kew, Daisy is still painting studiously when the door flies open and Rupert rushes in. Daisy looks up, startled. 'Rupert! You quite startled me.'

Rupert ignores her. 'Why didn't you tell me?'

'Tell you what?'

'That you are coming to live at Kew!'

'What are you on about?'

'You don't know?'

Daisy shakes her head. 'Know what?'

'Mr Banks just told me that they are cleaning out the cottage behind the orangery for you to move into when your sister goes to the country.'

Daisy look highly doubtful. 'That all sounds very well – but I'm not sure even Mr Banks has the authority to arrange that.'

'Perhaps not. But the Queen does!'

Daisy runs to the Queen's cottage, knocks on the door of the Queen's parlour and enters. The Queen is sitting talking with the countess. The pair stop and look up as

Daisy makes her obeisance to both women.

'My dear, did you not get my message that we would miss this afternoon's lesson?'

'Yes, Ma'am. But I wanted to come and thank you personally for arranging for me to come and live at Kew and for finding me accommodation. How can I ever repay you?'

'Shall we agree that it is my payment to you for the tuition? You have a place to live; the garden, and the kitchen will provide your food. When the King is not here, you are welcome to join me and the ladies-in-waiting for supper.'

'You are very kind, Ma'am.'

'It's always a pleasure to use the small influence I have for the benefit of another woman – we don't get much opportunity in this world of men.'

Daisy nods and drops a small curtsey.

'Anyway, it was the countess who went to the trouble of informing your family. I simply sat around musing on the world.'

The countess nods. 'Your brother-in-law is singularly unpleasant.'

'Yes, milady. I would go so far as to say he is bellicose.'

The Queen plays around with the word in her mind. 'Miss Salter, I can see your way with words is a match for your skill with the paintbrush.'

Gardner is pottering in the greenhouse at Godolphin House when Daisy enters. He looks up and nods.

'Well, Mr Gardner, I am to leave your excellent garden and move to Kew whilst Lady Fanny is away in the country.'

'I know, miss – my wife said. She has been told she will be going with you as your maid.'

'Maid? Why will I need a maid?'

'To look after you in your cottage, miss, and dress you in the evenings. You will be in the company of royalty. It is a great honour for my Kate.'

'But surely you will miss her?'

'Slaves get used to going without, miss.'

'You will be most welcome to visit.'

Gardner looks doubtful. 'I am not sure that would be appropriate, miss.'

Daisy tries to reassure him. 'All people care about at Kew is the garden. I shall ask Mr Masson if he can find you some work with the gardeners there.'

Daisy's new residence is pretty, and such is her standing with the garden staff, they have made a neat job of clearing it out and tidying it up. They have cut the grass, weeded and raked the gravel path, and pruned the roses. Two trees, a damson and a pear, hang heavy with fruit either side of the front door. The cottage is a good size but quite cosy with fires to keep the autumn and winter chills at bay and a kitchen with a range to cook on. Rupert crunches up the path with something under his arm. He knocks at the door. Kate opens it and shows him in.

Daisy, busy eating breakfast, looks up as Kate enters. 'Mr Fitzgerald, miss.'

Rupert follows her, looking nervous.

'Have you come for breakfast? I have a few chickens out the back, and we can probably spare you an egg.'

Rupert shakes his head.

Daisy continues eating. 'I thought you were off with Mr Masson?'

'I leave Kew tomorrow. We sail from Bristol this time next week. But I wanted to ask you something before I leave.' Rupert looks pointedly at Kate, and Daisy, catching the hint, dismisses her.

Once Kate is away, Daisy pushes away her plate and indicates he should sit. 'I am all ears.'

Rupert remains standing.

'I've brought something to show you.' He takes the envelope from under his arm and presents it to Daisy. It contains a painting of a daisy chain, with one daisy missing. Rupert looks on eagerly whilst Daisy considers it. 'What do you see? What do you think?'

'Rupert, it is quite charming, though I think you might have used a little more rose madder on the white of the petals.' She smiles at Rupert who looks frustrated.

'But do you see what it is?'

'It is a daisy chain.'

'But do you see what is missing?'

Daisy considers the painting. 'Other than a splash of madder?'

'Why can girls be so infuriating! There is a daisy missing!'

'So I see. Why did you do that?'

Rupert turns away and stomps to the window in frustration then turns around and stares at her. 'It's you who is missing. You are the missing Daisy!'

Daisy looks blank.

'You have become my life, my daisy chain. My voyage with Francis will be dangerous but, God willing, I will return safe – and when I do, will you complete the chain for me?' Rupert gets down on one knee. 'Miss Salter, when I return, will you do me the honour of becoming my wife?'

Daisy now stands and paces the room, looking at Rupert and looking away again. She takes the breakfast plates to the basin. She washes her hands slowly before picking up a towel, which she grips tightly as she motions for Rupert to stand.

'I have to tell you, Mr Fitzgerald, that the thought of marrying you has not crossed my mind. Then again, this is not a personal slight on you. The thought of marrying *any* man has not crossed my mind. I am not disposed to be the marrying kind. This is not a decision I care to make right now, but I will think on your request whilst you are on your travels, and we shall see how matters stand when you return.'

Rupert looks devastated. At that moment, there is a knock on the door, and Van der Humm enters with some drawings. 'Miss Salter, Mr Fitzgerald, am I disturbing a private moment?'

Daisy regains her composure. 'Not at all. Mr Fitzgerald has pressing business elsewhere.' She smiles at Rupert. 'Mr

Fitzgerald, please take care on your journey and return safely to us.'

An abject Rupert bows politely and leaves. Daisy turns to Van der Humm. 'Now, meinheer – are you here to tell me what decision has been made on the planting scheme?'

THE EARL OF CLONMEL

In a large room in a building in Whitehall, a distinguished-looking man in his fifties, sombrely but smartly dressed, is working behind a large desk, writing with a quill. There is a knock on the door; it opens and in walks Rupert. The man stands up, smiles, crosses the room, takes Rupert by both shoulders and looks him up and down.

'Hello, Father.'

'Rupert. Well come, well come. It's good to see you before you depart on this distinguished voyage of adventure of yours. Sit down.'

Clonmel retreats behind his desk and Rupert takes a seat in front of it. Clonmel pours wine and passes a glass over. 'How are your plans? Is there anything I can do to assist with your preparations?'

'Father, in your role as Head of Intelligence for the King—'

Clonmel raises his glass. 'I know you want to say spymaster.'

'Quite. I wondered if you might know something about a Dutchman called Van der Humm?'

'Indeed, the man's a complete rogue! We're keeping

an eye on him. Fingers in many pies, some are his own business, but he also works for a man called de Vries who runs the Dutch spy network here.'

'You let the Dutch spy on us?'

Clonmel looks at Rupert like he thinks his son is daft. 'Of course, in a selective sort of way. Keep your friends close, and your enemies closer. That sort of thing. Why do you want to know?'

'There's a girl I have met—'

'Ah, the Queen's lady-in-painting!' Rupert looks shocked. 'I'm not spying on you, my boy – your mother told me without prompting. That doesn't count.'

'Well, Van der Humm seems to have inveigled himself into her affections. But I don't trust him.'

'And rightly so! We're watching him because we think he's involved in smuggling tea into America. But he is also involved with your friend Daisy's brother-in-law in slave-trading – not illegal but, at the very least, distasteful. And if he's getting close to your friend Miss Salter, he's getting close to the Queen. I will have my men consider him all the more closely.'

Rupert looks miserable. 'What a time to be going away.'

'There's never a good time to go away when you have a rival in love, my boy. By coincidence, I must go to Bristol for reasons of my own, so I will be there to see you off.'

Being more southerly than Liverpool, Bristol takes a day's sailing off the triangular trade and avoids the Irish Sea, which can be treacherous at the best of times. On this blustery September day, a grand carriage pulls up on the busy quayside close to a ship's gangplank. Hugo and Daisy get out, followed wearily by Fanny, who has not had the best of journeys. The coachman and groom pull down Hugo's luggage and take it on board.

Hugo immediately walks across to where men are loading chests and boxes into the hold. He looks into one of the boxes and hefts it – Daisy notices that it lifts easily. Then, without looking back at the two women, he starts to walk off towards the gangplank. Fanny pulls him back.

'Take care to stay safe, husband.'

Hugo lifts his chin and looks down his nose at her with disdain. 'Give my regards to my brother. And be sure you give me an heir.' He boards the ship without a backwards glance.

Daisy gives Fanny a hug.

'Fanny, why on earth did we come all the way to Bristol for you to suffer that sort of dismissal!'

'You may find it strange, but he is my husband and I worry for him – and for my and Esme's future.' She pats her gravid belly. 'As it stands, if anything happens to Hugo, there is no heir, and if I have another girl…' She leaves the sentence dangling.

'That is exactly why I don't want a husband.'

The women watch as the crew weigh anchor and the ship sails. There is another ship behind. Masson and

Rupert are busily talking on deck. Daisy points excitedly. 'Look, it is Mr Masson's ship.'

'With that nice Mister Fitzgerald. I thought you and he were rather well suited, Daisy.'

Daisy waves, but Rupert and Masson go below as sailors start to unfurl the sails. Fanny waves too. 'It looks as if that ship has sailed.'

Daisy regards the departing stern ruefully. 'Yes. Perhaps I will come to wish it hadn't.'

They are about to get back in their carriage when they are approached by a distinguished-looking stranger who addresses Daisy. 'Good afternoon.' He bows politely. 'My name is Clonmel. I believe you are Miss Salter, one of the Queen's retinue alongside my wife?'

Daisy and Fanny both curtsey – Daisy deeply, Fanny less so due to her gravid condition. Daisy replies in the affirmative. 'I am, indeed, sir.'

'Tell me, Miss Salter, you have younger eyes than I. That previous ship that left harbour, the one you were waving off – when it got to the end of the channel did it turn to port or sail straight ahead?'

'Indeed sir,' Daisy replies. 'I believe it went straight ahead. May I ask why the interest?'

Clonmel points to the stern of Rupert's rapidly vanishing ship and leans forwards to speak as if in confidence. 'That vessel there is sailing for the Africas and has already tacked to port to head south. If the previous vessel was bound for the triangular trade route, why did it not follow the same course, I wonder? It is a conundrum indeed. I thank you ladies for your confirmation.'

Daisy looks pensive and speaks before he can walk away. 'If I might be so bold as to venture, my lord, there was something else I noticed that I thought was a little strange.'

Clonmel regards her with interest. 'Yes, I have heard you *notice* things. What was it?'

'When the sailors were loading boxes and chests onto the front ship, they made light work of it – it was almost as if the boxes were empty. I wondered why that might be?'

Clonmel tilts his head sideways, looks at Daisy, looks away to the hull of the vessel they can see vanishing over the horizon, then back to the two women. 'That is very astute, Miss Salter. I had not spotted that myself – it pays to have young eyes and a curious mind. I can only think it is some kind of subterfuge, designed to mislead the onlooker. You have given me much to think about.'

He bows to both women who curtsey in return. 'Thank you again, ladies. I wish you happy onward journeys. You to Rutland, I believe, Lady Godolphin? Good luck there – in my experience, it is a place bereft of charm.'

He turns and walks to his waiting carriage.

'Well, Daisy, he seems to know a lot about you and me,' Fanny muses.

Daisy watches the carriage turning off the quay for the London road. 'I am starting to suspect it might be his business to *know things*. I wonder why he was here.'

'Could he be an acquaintance of Mr Masson or Mr Fitzgerald, do you think?'

Daisy thinks for a moment. 'Not to my knowledge, Fanny. Not to my knowledge.'

THE PLANTING PARTY

The tulips duly arrive at Brentford Dock, and there is much excitement about putting them in the ground. With the sun shining on the ground where they are to be planted, Daisy, Van der Humm, Masson and Banks are in attendance to oversee the activity. All are dressed for a day's work, the men with their sleeves rolled up, Daisy in an apron with her hair tied back and wearing a straw hat.

Banks surveys the vista. 'I think we have agreed the perspective from the viewpoint should be due south towards the midday sun. Where exactly is north, do you think?'

Daisy rummages in her bag and takes out a small piece of silver and hands it to Banks. 'Mr Banks, I have a compass here.'

Banks takes the device and looks closely at it, looks at Daisy, looks back at the device and shows it to the others. 'It is a pocket sundial – and a truly magnificent one.' He demonstrates to the others. 'See, this small compass shows us north then we lift this "gnomon", and it tells us that it is… already around ten o'clock – we should make haste!'

He hands the device back to Daisy. 'You are a constant surprise, Miss Salter.'

'Thank you, sir, I have a marvellous collection of scientific devices – from my father.'

'Well, this one is fit for a king.'

As if on cue, they hear the sound of horses trotting and carriage wheels rumbling. All stop talking to look around as the barouche appears carrying the King and Queen. It stops a few yards from Banks and his companions. Footmen jump down and help the King, then a decidedly gravid Queen, to alight.

Banks and the other men bow low. Daisy makes the deepest curtsey possible in her apron and gardening boots.

The King looks expectant, and Banks rushes to make introductions. 'Your Majesty, Francis Masson you know, but I do not believe you have met Meinheer Van der Humm?'

The King nods. 'Meinheer, I understand we have you to thank for this great gift?' Van der Humm makes another deep bow. 'Well, consider yourself royally thanked!'

Banks turns to Daisy. 'And this is—'

The King interrupts him. 'I know who *this* is, Joseph. This is my Queen's lady-in-painting!' Daisy curtseys again, blushing all the more. 'It is a pleasure to meet you, Miss Salter – my wife speaks very highly of your skill. Indeed, I was most impressed by your... impressions.' The King smiles, and the men chuckle at the *bon mot*. 'I do think that style of work may well catch on.'

Daisy looks abashed. 'Impressionism, Your Majesty? I really cannot see it becoming all that popular.'

Both the Queen and the King regard her for a moment before the King speaks again. 'Well, Banks, what are you waiting for? I've only come to watch for a short while.'

Banks is about to give the orders to begin the planting when Daisy ventures to speak. 'Majesty?' The King looks at her enquiringly, Banks and the men look at her apprehensively. 'As the tulips are a personal gift to you and the Queen, would you like to help plant the first few?'

The King considers then breaks into a beaming smile. 'Well, Miss Salter, I must say that is a capital idea. Show me what I must do.'

'Certainly, Your Majesty. Cup your hands and turn your back to the field.' The King does as he is asked, and Daisy fills his hands with tulip bulbs. 'Now, simply fling them back over your head, and we'll plant them where they land.' She stands back to give the King space, and with great gusto, he hurls the tulips over his head.

The King looks at Banks. 'What do you say, Joseph – was that all right?'

Banks points to Daisy. 'Majesty, as this is all Miss Salter's idea, I cannot exactly say.'

The King raises an enquiring eyebrow in Daisy's direction. She is full of excitement. 'Majesty, that was truly excellent! I do not believe there is any other garden that can claim to have been planted under such direction by the royal hand.'

The King smiles. 'Well, Miss Salter, if you think that is the way it should be, perhaps I will stay and help for a little longer?'

Daisy can't help but clap her hands in delight, and all the men join in the applause. The King calls a footman to take his jacket, looks to the other men, sees how their sleeves are rolled up, does the same to his and sets to work.

Daisy turns to the Queen. 'Would you like to help, Ma'am?'

The Queen looks gleeful, and happily joins in, as does the countess and other members of the royal party.

Soon bulbs are flying everywhere, and whenever there is a lull, gardeners scurry forwards to plant them, four inches deep, as the royals look on.

The Queen quickly tires and goes to sit in the shade of a tree. At noon, the King sends the carriage back to the Kew kitchens with instructions to fetch food, and beer for the men and wine for the ladies.

The hungry workforce, royalty included, exchange tools and tulip bulbs for pies and bread with cheese, their strong appetites made of the open air. The gardeners are particularly pleased to be in such close proximity to their ruler, gawping as the King walks amongst them handing out words of encouragement along with their beer. It is a side of him they have never seen.

Lunch finished, it is time for the royal couple to head back to Kew, and the King seeks out Banks and Daisy as they are getting more bulbs ready for the afternoon session.

'Miss Salter, Joseph knows I am a keen agriculturalist, but this was the first time I have ever got my hands dirty in the soil – it was a liberating experience. More than that, it was good, honest fun! We royals do not have much time for fun, too much duty to do, you know. And what fun there is tends to be a contrivance. Then again, my wife did tell me that you were fun. Thank you, it has been a most enjoyable day.'

Daisy, who feels she has blushed enough in one morning for a whole year, blushes again, but she looks the King in the eye as she curtseys – thinking to herself that she is getting rather good at conducting the move on rough ground. 'Majesty, it was such an honour to work alongside you.'

The King looks mystified. 'Work? Well, I suppose it *was* work in a way. Perhaps work is fun then?' He looks thoughtful, then turns and walks back to the Queen and countess. As the barouche departs, the King and Queen wave farewells, and Banks' party and the gardeners wave back.

Planting recommences and everybody bustles around throwing tulip bulbs and giving instructions to gardeners. Throughout the afternoon, Van der Humm and Daisy work side-by-side chatting with lots of eye contact. The planting goes on until early evening, and when finally finished, Banks pours more beer for all the men, and wine for Daisy.

Everybody strolls back to the main buildings exhausted but happy, Daisy on Van der Humm's arm. 'Do you think any of the tulips might come up black, meinheer?' she asks.

'I think not. Your brother and I are still working on breeding the black variety. None of those planted today will be black.'

PICCADILLY

A few days later, Daisy is painting. There is a knock on her door, and Van der Humm enters. She puts down her brush and welcomes him warmly. 'This is a surprise, meinheer. I had not expected to see you for some time.'

'It's hard to stay away from a place of such... beauty.' He pauses to establish the double entendre. 'But I come with an invitation. Are you busy Friday at five o'clock?'

'Not that I know of, meinheer. The Queen has no lesson this Friday, so I have no commitments. What would you invite me to do?'

Van der Humm looks conspiratorial, something of an easy feat for a man of his particular talents. 'You know that Mr Banks is to be made President of the Royal Society?'

Daisy nods. 'Yes, it is in recognition of his eminence by his scientific peers.'

'He will be invested on Friday in Piccadilly. I have an invitation for the ceremony. Would you like to accompany me?'

Daisy is quite taken aback. 'Meinheer, you do me an honour. I would love to come.'

'The honour is mine. Shall I call for you in the courtyard

at half past three, and we will drive to Piccadilly together?'

Daisy rises and curtseys. 'That would be perfect.'

Van der Humm bows. 'Would you have time to walk in the garden with me now?'

Daisy takes off her painting apron. 'That sounds perfect too.'

Come Friday, Mr Banks obviously being otherwise engaged, Daisy finishes her work at lunchtime and returns to her cottage so Kate can help her dress for the outing. Kate is fixing Daisy's hair in front of the dressing table mirror when she notices her mistress looking thoughtful.

'Is everything all right with you, miss?'

'Could I ask you something, Kate?'

'Of course, miss. Anything.'

'How did you know you were in love?'

Kate is now buttoning up the back of Daisy's dress. 'Take a deep breath please, miss.'

Daisy regards her quizzically. 'Is it that serious?'

'No, miss, the deep breath is so I can do the fastenings here.' She punctuates her reply with each button finding its fastening. 'Well, miss,' *button*. 'There have been many ways,' *button*. 'Because I thought I was in love more than once,' *button*. 'And,' *button*. 'If you think you are,' *button*. 'That's often enough to go on at the beginning,' *button*. 'There. You can breathe out now.'

Daisy exhales and relaxes her shoulders. 'And what kind of things would make you think you are… in love?' She turns round on the stool to face Kate.

'Ooh, let me see… If your heart beats faster when you see a gentleman. When he happens to touch your hand and your skin feels as if it's on fire. When you know you dare not look at the gentleman, for fear of blushing from the roots of your hair to your toenails. When the man is the last thing you think of at night, and the first thing you think of in the morning – although that can come from eating too much cheese!'

'You blush, Kate?'

'Of course, miss. All women blush.' Her eyes twinkle. 'Except, with my colour skin, it's harder for a man to see – which means we don't give so much away!'

'You sound very coquettish, Kate. But tell me, how did you choose between these men?'

Kate gets Daisy to stand and straightens her skirts. 'That was easy, miss. Lots of men had flirted with me, and made suggestions, and some had even offered to marry me, and I'd always said no.' Kate pauses to fiddle with a hem.

'Go on, don't tease me.'

Kate stands up and looks Daisy in the eye, head on one side, slightly wistfully. 'Well, when my husband… having never flirted with me… nor made a suggestion other than we might go for a walk to the river… and even then, still not touching me… and talking most of the time about gardening and melons… but always looking me straight in the eye… and asking my opinions, and listening to them… When he asked me to marry him… I couldn't help myself but say yes.'

Daisy is all sympathy. 'Oh Kate, how you must miss your Mr Gardner.'

'I do, miss. But I see him at chapel where we black people worship every Sunday. And I know he's not going anywhere and nor am I. We will be together again, and he is always in my heart and I in his.'

'But how did you get him to ask you? I've no practice at batting my eyes, and simpering and swooning and giggling, and… and looking helpless.'

Kate smiles. 'Don't you worry about that, miss. I've looked after simpering ladies who come to stay at Godolphin House. I must say most men quickly find it very tedious and tire of such affectations.'

'But you still do not answer my question!'

'It's a question of time, miss. Give a man time and silence, and he'll come round to thinking of it and asking. Keep talking and batting your eyelids, and he gets distracted.'

'You make it sound so simple, Kate.'

'Most men are simple, miss. There, you look a picture. Now, all you have to do is wait for the man who makes you smile and catch your breath, and makes your heart beat faster, to wrap himself around you like a vine. Stand still, though – no point in making him chase any harder than he already thinks he is!'

'I have never yet met a man who makes my heart beat faster. That doesn't sound at all scientific. Walking up a hill – yes. But a man…?' Daisy purses her lips as Kate picks up the Floris bottle and looks at her enquiringly. Daisy nods agreement.

That afternoon, Piccadilly is busier than ever, and Daisy and Van der Humm have to join a queue to get into the presentation.

'Daisy, you claim to be a woman of science, what do you know of this society?'

Daisy, who has heard all about it from her father, stands in front of Van der Humm and puts her hands together, assuming the grin of a cheeky schoolgirl about to present a well-rehearsed lesson. 'The Royal Society of London for Improving Natural Knowledge received Royal Assent in 1663 and owes its origins to a lecture given by Christopher Wren, at Gresham College in Barnard's Inn off High Holborn, in 1660.'

Van der Humm smiles. 'I'm impressed.'

Daisy puts a finger up to quieten him. 'Wait, there is more. The list of members, or Fellows, is a veritable pantheon of scientific greats and polymaths. Robert Boyle and John Wilkin were founders. The Society published Isaac Newton's *Principia Mathematica* and Mr Benjamin Franklin's kite experiment. It is the foremost scientific institution in the world.'

Van der Humm continues to look impressed. 'But how does Joseph Banks rate in importance in this exalted company?'

Since working at Kew, Daisy has made a thorough study of Joseph Banks. 'Well, meinheer, Mr Banks was educated at Harrow, Eton and Oxford and was elected a Fellow of the Royal Society in 1766 when he was very young. He really made his reputation when the Society supported his voyage, on *Endeavour* captained by James

Cook, to plot the transit of Venus in Tahiti, and later to voyage to Australia and claim the territory as British. Although I *have* heard rumours at Kew, from the Queen, that Mr Banks, who for one seemingly so humble is a man of significant wealth, contributed £10,000 towards the costs of the voyage for himself and his companion scientists.'

Van der Humm looks even more impressed. 'Miss Salter, you have truly researched your topic.'

Daisy looks a little smug. 'As any scientist would, meinheer!'

The courtyard of the Royal Society bustles with men of science jostling to get in. Van der Humm presents his ticket at the door; they go inside and are directed to seats with a good view of the stage. Banks is sitting on the stage with other Fellows of the Society. An official-looking man is talking at a lectern.

'The officers of the Royal Society, determining that Joseph Banks is the foremost scientist of our time, do duly elect him and welcome him as President of our most esteemed institution.'

Banks steps forwards and the official puts a chain around his neck to much clapping and murmurs of appreciation. The official invites him to the lectern to speak.

'My fellow scientists. I thank you for this accolade, which in large part has come about by the serendipity of being in the right place at the right time with the right people around me. I accept this honour, not just for myself, but on behalf of the many men and, may I say, women of science'—at this point, he notices Daisy in the audience and nods, causing many in the audience to look around and notice her for the first time—'who will go on to make the discoveries of the future. We must all brook no obstacle in advancing scientific thinking and opinion properly supported by observation and evidence. *Nullius in Verba*!'

With applause for Banks still ringing in their ears, Daisy and Van der Humm emerge into the foyer where waiters are handing out cordial. Van der Humm nods and speaks to a few people, introducing Daisy as Kew Gardens' Painter in Residence. She is surprised how many learned men are happy to converse with her and take an interest in her role.

In one such conversation with three other men, Van der Humm asks a question to them all. 'Do any of you gentlemen know Latin? We Dutch tend not to, and I was wondering what Mr Banks' last words, *Nullius in Verba* mean?'

The men hesitate, but Daisy responds immediately. 'It is the Society's motto, meinheer. It means "Take nobody's word for it" – it is an instruction to men of science to believe their own eyes and the proof of demonstrable experiment.'

'Quite so, Miss Salter, but not just *men* of science,' comes a voice over Daisy's shoulder. It is Banks, wearing his chain of office, who has caught the conversation as he was circling the room.

Daisy looks questioningly at him. 'There is more, sir?'

Banks nods affirmatively. 'As I said from the lectern,

we must consider women of science too.'

Some of the men gathered around guffaw, but Banks silences them with a stern look. 'Gentlemen, science is not only the remit of the male sex. Miss Salter here, whilst she is yet young, is in possession of one of the best scientific and enquiring minds I have conversed with in many years. Certainly, she takes nobody's word for it – or at least no man's.'

Daisy blushes to her roots. The men chuckle but look doubtful and amble off.

Banks lets them go. 'Miss Salter, meinheer. This is a pleasure. How do you come to be here?'

'I am meinheer's guest, sir, and I am delighted to be in the privileged position to offer my congratulations in person on such an auspicious day.'

Banks smiles appreciatively and looks to Van der Humm.

'My government received an invitation, sir, and knowing of our acquaintance asked me to come as their representative.'

Banks raises an eyebrow. 'Ambassadorial duties, meinheer?'

'Not entirely that grand, sir, but on behalf of the people of Holland, may I offer you our congratulations – a scientist of your eminence is well-deserving of the position.'

Banks nods and moves on.

Daisy gently touches Van der Humm on the arm. 'I did not know you had government connections, meinheer – I thought you were a bulb merchant?'

'He looks at where her hand is resting and smiles at her. 'There are a lot of things about me you do not yet know.'

'All good things, I hope. Meinheer, you become ever more intriguing.'

Daisy smiles, as does Van der Humm. But when she moves her gaze to look at all the people at the gathering, his eyes slide away.

Interest in the throng exhausted, Daisy refocuses on her companion. 'Now, sir, I have never been to the very centre of London, and I am hungry. I do hope you've planned to buy me dinner somewhere extravagant?' She looks at him wide-eyed. Feeling brazen. Wondering what Kate would say and hoping she would approve.

Van der Humm is happily back on solid ground. 'I know just the place in St. James's. Just around the corner from Floris, in fact.'

DOGGET O'FLYNN

HMS *Resolution*, under the stewardship of Captain James Cook, arrives in the Dutch Cape Colony some 120 years after it was founded as a layover port for ships en route to the Orient. It is 30 October, 110 days since the ship left home waters, and as their vessel cruises south, Table Mountain heaves into view. Getting ever closer, they see the bristle of masts on vessels of all shapes and sizes nestled against the wharves in the distance. Rupert and Masson stand side-by-side at the rail as the captain brings the ship alongside the quay and sailors throw lines ashore to matelots waiting to make *Resolution* fast around buoys.

'What did you think to your first sea voyage, Rupert?' Masson asks.

Rupert grimaces. 'Fine enough once the sickness stopped. I liked it best when we went ashore. Madeira was particularly lovely.'

'Aye, fair enough,' Masson agrees. 'Although, by the time we made the Cape Verde islands, I felt as rocky ashore as I did on the deck. The ground wouldn't stay still.'

The two men smile at one another, bonding over the passage. 'Anyway, Francis, I expect we'll have time to find our land legs again. I'm looking forward to a decent meal, a glass of wine and a soft bed tonight.'

Cook has walked across to join them and extends a hand. 'It's goodbye then, gentlemen, you'll easily find lodgings somewhere along the waterfront. I hope your "hunt" goes well. Joseph Banks seemed very excited by what he discovered when we hove-to here for ten days on our return with the *Endeavour*.'

Masson shakes his hand warmly. 'Thank you, sir, on behalf of myself, Mr Fitzgerald and indeed Mr Banks. We have letters of introduction from Mr Banks to a Swedish botanist called Carl Thunberg who will hopefully make us welcome here.'

Cook muses briefly. 'Thunberg? Yes, he came on board *Endeavour* to meet Joseph. Nice man, well-educated and with an easy humour. Talked non-stop about botany – you'll get on well!' He turns and leaves to shout at some sailors.

Rupert and Francis oversee the unloading of their bags and various empty packing cases brought on the voyage specially to take care of specimens. They follow them down the gangplank, engage a man with a handcart and walk off along the waterfront to find suitable lodgings.

After a good meal, a good night's rest, breaking their fast on plates of ham and eggs washed down by the bitter Dutch coffee, they walk half a mile or so inland from the quay. Asking directions several times amidst the jumble of streets and alleyways, they finally come across a substantial house standing back from the rutted track that passes for a road, stroll up the drive and knock on the door. It is opened by a tall, scholarly-looking man of some thirty years, hair scraped back, wearing a brocade waistcoat and wire-rimmed glasses perched on his nose, over which he peers enquiringly.

Masson takes a letter from his pocket. 'Francis Masson and Rupert Fitzgerald from His Majesty's royal botanical gardens at Kew.' Both he and Rupert bow with deep respect. 'I bring a letter of introduction from Joseph Banks.'

The tall man nods at them, regards the letter and smiles broadly. 'Yes, indeed, I recognise the hand. We spent some days together during his visit here, annotating plant specimens and making notes. Welcome, gentlemen. I am Carl Thunberg, do please come in.'

He takes them through to a study where the walls are lined with drawings and paintings of plants that Rupert and Masson regard with interest, raising eyebrows and pointing at some of the more unearthly specimens. Thunberg lets them look for a moment or two before waving them to seats. 'The Eastern Cape, gentlemen, is a rich source of surprises. As you are come in spring, I can only assume you are thinking of an expedition to see what you can collect.'

'You read us perfectly, sir,' Masson replies. 'I come here with a brief to see the Cape through all four seasons and make visits to the interior during each to collect plants and seeds and take notes.'

Thunberg looks at Rupert with an arched brow. 'And you, Rupert, what is your role?'

Rupert looks slightly embarrassed. Masson speaks

for him. 'Excuse his confusion, sir, for I have not yet told him exactly why he is here.' He smiles encouragingly at Rupert who is looking even more perplexed. 'In part, he is here to help me, of course, but in particular, Mr Banks has been charged by His Majesty King George to try and find, in his own words, a plant fit for a queen, to give to Her Majesty on her birthday. If we find something of suitable magnificence, Rupert is to take the first available ship back to England in all haste.'

Thunberg grins and gestures to the paintings on his walls, most of which are of succulent plants and others that would grow in arid landscapes. 'I would imagine these are not entirely the sort of things you have in mind?'

Masson nods towards Rupert who finally opens his mouth and speaks. 'Whilst they are most interesting, sir, I would venture they are rather too spiky for our queen, who is altogether more soft and feminine.'

Thunberg claps his hands in delight. 'Well said, Rupert, well said. In that case, we will have to see what we can do to assist.' He stands up and paces towards a big bay window. 'Normally, gentlemen, nothing would give me greater pleasure than to accompany you on such an adventure. However, I am to take ship next week to visit my tutor and mentor Carl von Linné who is old and unwell.'

Rupert looks awestruck. 'You studied under Carolus Linnaeus?' Thunberg nods. Rupert sighs and shakes his head. 'The greatest botanist the world has ever known. I studied some of his texts at Oxford. What is he like in person?'

Thunberg takes a watch from his waistcoat pocket, opens it and checks the time. 'Why don't I tell you over lunch?'

The three men leave the house, and Thunberg walks them back to the waterfront, where he leads the way towards an inn sign brandishing a beast with long, pronged horns. Thunberg is amused by the manner in which the two men regard it.

'That, gentlemen, is an antelope called a kudu, for which the inn is named. Most of the meat you'll find in the Cape is served in the Dutch fashion – mostly pork or goat with heavy sauces. The host at the Kudu is one of my countrymen who likes the local meat served plain and simple. He has good connections with the natives, and his cellar is stocked with some excellent local Cape wines – in my opinion, there is only so much genever a man can drink, although the Dutch would have you think different.'

They are shown to a table, and the Scotsman and the Irishman happily let the Swede order. The food is wholesome and tasty, and the wine is surprisingly good. Masson swills it around his glass and admires the deep colour. 'If nothing else, Rupert, you must take some vine cuttings back for the Kew greenhouses. It would be interesting to see if we can do as well.'

Thunberg tops up the glasses. 'Let's talk business. I cannot come with you, but I have a man who has accompanied me into the interior on most of my trips. He knows the country, gets on well with the natives and has become quite adept at spotting plants.'

Masson looks interested. 'He's a safe man to travel with?'

'More to the point, Francis, he will definitely keep you safe. He's an interesting sort, a little older than me. If his accounts are true, he was something of a soldier of fortune. But if ever you were looking for a man to take into the jungle with you – not that you'll find any jungle around here – he would be the one.'

Masson raises his glass in salute. 'I look forward to meeting him. What's he called?'

'Dogget O'Flynn.'

Masson sits back in his chair. 'Interesting name?'

Thunberg looks at him steadily. 'Interesting man.'

Rupert's ears prick up. 'O'Flynn? Must have some Irish blood in him. Be good to have a fellow countryman along the way.'

Thunberg looks doubtful. 'Don't expect too much – he came here from the colonies in America. I wouldn't even be sure O'Flynn is his real name. And he has the sort of scars on his back that I've only ever seen before on slaves from the plantations.'

Masson puts down his glass and raises his eyebrows. 'He's of African descent?'

'No. He's as white as you and I, although his skin betrays his time in hot sun. As I said, he's interesting, unusual even. Educated, yet somehow almost feral at the same time. There are tales there that may be better left untold.'

Rupert is intrigued. 'When will we meet him?'

'At my house, ten-thirty tomorrow morning.'

The following day, Rupert and Masson retrace their steps to Thunberg's house. He welcomes them and takes them to his study. As they enter, a man unwinds from a chair by the window. He has a shock of curly black hair and skin turned the colour of a walnut by the sun. He wears his moustache and beard in the Dutch fashion, groomed to a neat point, against which his teeth flash white as he smiles. Lines surround his eyes – whether from looking too much at the sun or from laughing, Rupert and Masson cannot be sure.

His eyes are as green as the leaves on a holly wreath. Eyes that measure and assess. He is tall in stature, wearing a white shirt and tan breeches tucked into leather boots in the colonial style. He shakes hands with Masson and Rupert in turn. His grip is firm and cool.

'My name is Dogget. Carl says that you are looking for a guide to accompany you on an expedition to discover plants and flowers.' His voice is deep and resonant containing an amused smile. 'Provided we can come to an accommodation over my retainer for the journey, I am happy to be that guide.'

Masson looks at him. 'You know the territory?'

O'Flynn doesn't answer at first. He turns his hands over and starts regarding his nails before looking up. 'Mr Masson, I know it like the back of my hand.'

DAMSON JAM

Late summer at Kew is the same as in any garden, no matter how grandiose – a time when the flowers droop as the plants set seed and the garden comes to fruition. Thoughts of landscaping and planting are set aside for the harvest, and there is much work to be done in the kitchen, preserving fruit for the coming winter. Thus it is, that as Daisy walks to the Queen's cottage, there is a mystifying clinking-chinking sound coming from the basket swinging gently in her hand.

She finds the Queen in her parlour with the countess and a wet nurse who is feeding the Queen's most recent family addition, Prince Ernest. The Queen looks up. 'I did not think we were due to paint today?'

'Ma'am, Countess, I rather hoped you might take part in a scientific experiment?' She looks at them excitedly. As is only proper, the Queen speaks first.

'Science? What do we know of science and experiments?' The countess nods agreement. 'But we are all ears – tell us more: am I to be the experiment?'

'Oh no, certainly not, Ma'am. This is the experiment.'

Daisy reaches into her basket, brings out a freshly baked loaf of bread, knives, three plates, three jars filled with a dark purple confection and three tiny spoons. 'I would like you to try my damson jam.'

The countess, who has been looking doubtful, perks up. 'Jam? Well, it won't be an experiment for me to eat jam – I have years of practice and must say I'm rather good at it! But that loaf smells wonderful, and I do think it sounds like a very good idea.' She looks pensive. 'Of course – we must have tea too!'

The two older women laugh, and a footman is sent for tea whilst Daisy cuts slices of bread, which she puts on the plates, passing them over with knives before opening all three jars and carefully placing a spoon in each.

'It will be fun, Your Majesty, Countess, but trust me, it *is* an experiment. Whilst these are all jars of damson jam, made from damsons picked from a tree that grows beside my studio, they are all made with different sweeteners. One is made with sugar from the Indies, one is made with my own honey, and the third is made with sugar from beets, which I got from the royal kitchen – the cook tells me His Majesty the King has been very interested in the planting of beets in Suffolk and Norfolk.'

The Queen was instantly engaged by the conversation. 'You keep bees? I've always wanted to keep bees; they seem so happy buzzing through the roses around my door.'

'Yes, Ma'am. When the gardeners were cleaning out the cottage you so kindly provided, they found a few old straw bee skeps that had been stored there. They were going to throw them onto a fire, but I rescued them and then found the Royal Beekeeper who had some new queens that were about to swarm, and he gave them to me.'

The Queen looks wistful. 'Hmm, queens swarming.' She regards her youngest prince. 'Sounds a bit like me – perhaps I should get the King to build me a hive.'

The brief awkward silence is broken by the countess. 'Did you know we had a Royal Beekeeper, Ma'am?'

The Queen shakes her head.

'I don't think it's a real title, your ladyship,' Daisy tells her, trying to bring the subject back to jam. 'It's just how the people in the garden and the kitchen refer to him. But he is certainly a very "sweet" man.'

Daisy makes the quip with wide, innocent eyes and waits. As the penny drops, both women burst out laughing and the humour returns as the countess reaches for the nearest jam jar. 'Does it matter which one first?'

Daisy cuts her slice of bread into three equal pieces, and the women follow her lead, spooning a different jam onto each piece. Before they can start, they hear a knock at the door, and a servant ushers in Banks who bows. He sees the various jars and patterns of bread on the table and looks bemused.

The Queen points to the spread. 'Ah, Mr Banks, as a man of science and President of the Royal Society, you can obviously see what we're doing here.'

Banks studies the table quizzically. 'As a man of science, I'd say you were eating bread and jam, Your Majesty.'

The countess joins in. 'No such thing, Mr Banks. Miss Salter has engaged us in a scientific experiment regarding damson jam.'

Whilst not a man normally out of his depth, Banks looks confused. 'A scientific experiment? With jam?'

Daisy has prepared Banks a plate of bread and jam and hands it to him. 'I looked at three sorts of sugar under my microscope – cane sugar, honey and the King's new beet sugar – and they were all very different. So, I made three lots of jam from them to see how they would alter the taste.'

Banks is now the centre of attention and, as befits the President of the Royal Society when faced with a scientific challenge, he composes his face and tastes each sample, chewing well, taking a good swallow of tea in between. The women regard him keenly. Banks draws himself up and looks at them each in turn.

'Well, I am but one opinion, and in science, we have to have a consensus. What do you ladies think?'

The countess guffaws. 'My word, Banks, you're not a politician – give us your opinion.'

Banks looks down at his plate, then up at Daisy. 'Well, Miss Salter, in my *opinion*, they are all delicious.'

The Queen realises he is teasing them and chuckles. 'Get on with it, man – you can take that as a royal command!'

Banks bows. 'Your Majesty, I do believe the one in the middle is my favourite. It tempers the sharpness of the *Prunus insititia* without being cloying. The one on the right is a little heavy and the one on the left a bit, shall we say, less inspiring. Whilst all remain delicious.'

Everybody looks at Daisy in expectation. 'Well, Your Majesty, Countess, sir, I think the King will be very pleased as that is the one made using his beet sugar, newly come from Norfolk.'

The countess nods her agreement. The Queen claps her hands. 'That is my view exactly! Daisy, if you do not mind, I would very much like to try this experiment on His Majesty myself – may I have these three pots?'

Daisy drops her lowest curtsey – she has got rather good at it over the past months. 'It would be my honour for the King to taste my jam, Ma'am. After all, they are his damsons too.'

Everybody is keen to repeat the experiment. So it is, after more bread and jam and tea, that Daisy finds herself walking back through the garden with a thoughtful Banks.

'I didn't know you had a microscope, Daisy?'

'It was my father's, sir.'

'Do you use it often?'

'Indeed, sir. And all the more for being here. I look at seeds and the details of petals and sepals on the plants, and anthers and stamens. It informs my paintings.'

Banks considers for a moment. 'Yes, that makes sense. But why did you think of using it to examine sugar?'

Daisy stops and looks at him. 'Curiosity firstly, sir. But the thing is, Mr Banks, when you look at things that closely, what might seem the same may turn out to be completely different. It's a way of determining the truth.'

Banks looks at her with appreciation and nods thoughtfully. They walk on until Banks bids her good evening as she turns along the path to her cottage.

The season of mellow fruitfulness progresses as ever in the northern hemisphere. The nights draw in, fires are lit early in greenhouses then, as the days grow colder, in hearths and ranges, in stately houses and cottages alike. Dew lays heavy on the grass, leaves turn to amber and gold, fall from the trees and are eagerly swept up by gardeners and groundsmen and squirreled away in wooden bins to rot down to mulch for next season.

Squirrels in their turn collect nuts and seeds to store over winter before finally retiring to the comfort of their dreys to hibernate. Under lowering clouds, lashed by rain squalls drumming on greenhouse windows, even Kew looks bereft. Daisy has to light candles in her studio from the moment she starts in the morning until she snuffs them out before retiring to her cottage for supper. Much of her painting now is of seed cases and seeds, and succulents from the cold greenhouses that do not suffer for the change in temperature and light.

Despite the gloom of winter, Daisy maintains her schedule of appointments with the Queen, focusing on painting the fruits harvested from the gardens and the exotic pineapples that come packed in straw from the colonies.

Van der Humm visits two or three times a week, coming either to Daisy in her studio or, on fine weekends, accompanying her on walks along the Thames towpath with Kate as chaperone. Often, he brings her things of interest – a book, a sweetmeat, a trinket he has picked up in London, a pair of gloves to keep her hands warm.

In the way of women, even royalty, the Queen and the

countess take delight in teasing Daisy.

'Your Majesty,' asks the countess one day, sewing whilst Daisy and the Queen are painting. 'What do you know of Holland?'

'I know it is somewhere between where I come from, and where I am now,' the Queen replies without looking up. 'I remember I travelled across it on my journey to take ship to England for my marriage to the King.'

'I'm told it is often called the low country, Your Majesty,' the countess says.

'Not only low, but very flat,' the Queen confirms.

Daisy is studying a pineapple and studiously ignoring the conversation.

'So would you say, Majesty,' the countess continues, 'that the Dutch people are beneath us?'

'That is a good question, countess. Not beneath us, but almost certainly below us.'

Daisy finally can take no more. 'But some Dutchmen are much taller than us. Surely that must compensate?'

The countess looks thoughtful. 'Yes, I suppose, say, in the case of Meinheer Van der Humm, if he was a horse, and measured in hands, he would be some hands taller than you?'

Daisy nods.

The Queen smiles, guessing what is coming next. 'In that case,' says the countess, pouncing, 'he must indeed be a *handsome* man?'

Daisy looks up, colouring slightly. 'Some might think so, milady. There are many more men in London, and indeed in Kew, than in the countryside where I come from.

Alas, I do not have enough experience however to judge them by their looks.'

The Queen breaks the ensuing silence. 'We have a saying in Germany – *gutaussehend ist wie gutaussehend*.'

The other women look on mystified.

'It translates into English,' said the Queen, 'as "handsome is as handsome does"!'

'Indeed,' says the countess. 'I would rather a kind man who was not so handsome, than a handsome man who was not so kind.'

Daisy looks thoughtful. The Queen reaches out and pats her hand. 'Of course, my dear, there is no reason why a man cannot be both.'

Daisy sits up straight and starts to pack her brushes away. 'That sounds excellent advice, Majesty. Should I ever need to consider men, or a man even, I will bear in mind what you have said. For the time being, however, it is far from being uppermost in my mind.'

She stands, curtseys to both women, and leaves. The Queen and the countess smile knowingly at each other.

PLANT HUNTING

utumn in England is spring on the Cape. With O'Flynn's help, Masson and Rupert have acquired horses, mules and carts for their expedition into the interior, along with a Dutch servant and a native guide. The weather as they head into the hills that sweep down to the ocean is clement, fresher than along the coast. Having climbed steadily all day, on the first evening they make camp up on a bluff above a pool in a fast-running stream.

O'Flynn sets the driver and guide to erect tents and start a fire, then invites the others to join him in a swim to wash the dust away. Masson turns down the offer, saying he is 'horse weary'. Rupert, more used to riding, willingly accepts.

The pair wander down to the river. O'Flynn strips off and wades in, causing Rupert to catch his breath and stare at the other man's back. The sun-darkened skin is covered in a cicatrix of scar tissue, light in places, darker in others, puckered and rough. Rupert dives in and gasps, enjoying the chill of the water and the freedom of swimming naked. Climbing out, the pair sit down to dry on the warmth of a flat rock.

Rupert gestures to O'Flynn's back. 'Very organic design you have on your skin, rather like ivy growing up from your waist to your shoulders.'

O'Flynn looks him in the eye. 'I thought ivy was poisonous?'

'It can be. That looks like it must have stung a bit?'

'It was a long time ago. Luckily, it is impossible to remember the sordid depths of abject pain, even that derived from being horsewhipped – in the same way as it is impossible to remember the ecstasy of extreme pleasure.'

Rupert looked thoughtful. 'The difference being, I imagine, that you never want to repeat the one whilst you cannot get enough of the other?'

'Although the other can always lead to the pain of a broken heart.' O'Flynn puts his head on one side and grins. 'However, all pain passes with time.'

'You've known both? I have never been whipped but believe I may be in the thrall of the latter.'

'Yes, I've known both. And I have escaped from both. But come, I am hungry, and supper smells good.'

The two men dress, head back to camp and are soon enjoying a rich stew watching the sun set over the distant sea. As the stars start to twinkle, O'Flynn breaks out a bottle of dark, smoky Cape rum and splashes it into tin mugs.

Masson takes a deep swig. 'Well, it's not Scotch whisky, but when travelling abroad, a man should be prepared to make compromises, and I've made many worse than this.' He raises his mug in salute. 'Mr O'Flynn, Mr Thunberg told us you had come to Cape Town from the American colonies. How did you find it there?'

'Brutal.'

Having seen O'Flynn's back, Rupert nods knowingly.

Masson wants to know more. 'You were born in the colonies?'

O'Flynn takes a long draught of his rum, picks up the bottle, pulls out the cork with his teeth and splashes more into his mug. 'You're an inquisitive man, Mr Masson.'

Masson stares across the fire at him. 'Aye, some would say that's the scientist in me, always seeking to improve my knowledge.' He shrugs disarmingly. 'Then again, we're to be together around a campfire for some nights to come, and it seems you are likely to be the one with the best stories.'

O'Flynn stares up at the stars, considering. He looks from Masson to Rupert and back again. He makes up his mind.

'Very well, I'll tell you a story of mine every evening. But you must tell me something in return – I'm very keen to hear about London as I'm eager to visit one day.'

Rupert reaches for the rum bottle. 'Suits me. Although I'm not quite sure what Francis can tell you about London – he's a dour Scotsman from a dour place called Scotland for which "dreich" is the best description!'

O'Flynn is confused. 'Dreich, what's that?'

Masson cheerily raises his mug. 'Dreich is also known as "that wee rain what gets you wet". I can tell you a lot about rain!'

O'Flynn looks no more enlightened. Rupert continues.

'Anyway, I think that, as we shall be together for a time, first names should be in order. So, Dogget, if I may call you that, you go first.'

By day, they travel deeper into the mountains collecting specimens and seeds. Late afternoons, they stop for Masson to update his meticulous notes. Sometimes, Rupert heads off with Dogget for a swim, or to hunt for supper. Other times, he borrows Masson's watercolours to paint or draw plants they have seen or collected. Having watched over Daisy's shoulder so often, he is becoming a proficient artist.

By night, they tell tales around the fire. Thus, they piece together that Dogget had been brought up an orphan on a tobacco plantation.

'I was so young I only vaguely remember my mother,' he tells them. 'But I have been told that she died when I was two. The only thing I have from my past is a locket containing a miniature, I suppose, of her, and some papers written in a language nobody seems to understand.'

Masson and Rupert are disconcerted by the sad tale. Rupert takes a swig of rum and is first to respond.

'You make the colonies sound most unpleasant.'

'Unless you are wealthy, they are atrocious, as was my upbringing. From the moment I could walk, I was set to work in the fields. But I grew strong, I was intelligent, and the overseers started to appreciate my value in managing the other slaves. That was until I was caught with an overseer's daughter who was teaching me to read and write. It was innocent, but I was whipped to within an inch of my life. Of course, slaves are valuable assets, so they made sure to keep me alive.

'Then it went beyond innocent – it was the overseer's daughter who nursed my whipped back, and we fell in love. Amelie hated her father for the way I had been treated, and after I had recovered, she started making plans for us to escape together. She contrived a ruse to visit a cousin living several plantations away, near the coast. Her cousin was to arrange passage for us on a ship to a country called Ireland.'

Dogget pauses to ask if either Rupert or Francis have heard of such a place. This leads to a lengthy digression as Rupert regales them with stories from his homeland.

Finally, Dogget resumes his tale. 'It is my experience that very few things succeed as planned. Hotly pursued by her father's men, we made it to the ship and set sail. Amelie had money, and she paid the ship's captain to marry us. We had a blissful two weeks of love and passion before my beloved bride caught a fever. The captain turned us off the ship in Boston where we found lodgings, but shortly after, I found myself a widower.'

O'Flynn turns away, looking into the distance. Rupert uncorks a second bottle of rum, recharges the glasses and waits patiently in silence.

'Distraught and virtually penniless, I signed on to a Portuguese merchant ship plying the reverse passage to Cape Verde carrying whale oil. Seafaring came naturally to me, and because I was good with other men and quickly learned the ropes, I soon became first mate.'

Masson and Rupert raise their glasses in salute.

'Having been a slave myself, and appreciating the value of human life, I had an extreme distaste for the middle passage. Luckily, I was able to persuade my captain of the benefits he would reap from not overloading and getting the human cargo across the Atlantic in good health. The money he earned was better, and other captains soon followed suit.

'I was not profligate, and as soon as I had acquired sufficient wealth, I found a ship sailing south to the Cape looking for a mate. I made the journey, bought a house and settled down to decide what to do next. My big hope is to get to England to tell the true stories of slavery and hopefully join the cause to get the filthy trade abolished.'

He smiled. 'In the meantime, I am happy escorting visitors like you two gentlemen into the interior.'

As is only fitting reward for a man telling such an interesting tale, mugs are again replenished. In return, Rupert regales Dogget with stories of London, the Court of King George, Kew Gardens, how society works, and how the country is looking to be heading for war with America in the near future.

Masson listens on with interest, but being closer in age, it is the two younger men who make firm friends.

THE BIRD OF PARADISE

After travelling for two months, wending back towards the coast, expecting to be in Cape Town within the next week or so, Masson spends the afternoon checking their collection and his notebooks. Joining the others for the customary pre-prandial rum, he seems slightly downbeat.

'Are you happy with what we have seen and collected so far?' Dogget asks, splashing spirit into a mug, and handing it to him.

Masson stretches. Like the others, after the past weeks of hard travelling, he is looking leaner and sharper featured. 'Well, gentlemen, I feel we have all but exhausted the flora in these higher reaches of the territory and have yet to find something to meet the King's brief.'

Dogget raises an enquiring eyebrow. Rupert takes up the narrative. 'If you recall, the King wishes us to find a unique and beautiful plant he can dedicate to Queen Charlotte and name after her.'

Dogget shouts to the native guide to come and join them, and they exchange words in the local dialect. The guide nods, looks excited and gesticulates in the direction of the sea, smiling broadly.

'Whatever he's excited about, I hope it's something we can all share in?' Masson enquires.

Dogget pats the smiling guide on the shoulder. 'He says that as we get nearer to the coast, where the rains fall more often, the plants are more like a beautiful woman than a withered old man, standing tall and elegant. He wants to take us to a place he knows of, two or three days' travel away, to show us a plant that reminds him of his wife – well, one of them anyway as he has three!'

'Poor man, no wonder he wants to get away from home and trek the hills,' conjectures Masson.

Rupert laughs out loud. 'I must say, Francis, on the basis that men like you will never marry, some chap has to have more than one wife, if only to give Mother Nature a chance to keep the planet populated.'

The guide looks perplexed, so Dogget translates the gist of the exchange – now it is the turn of the guide to burst into whoops of laughter. He points at Masson and speaks rapid-fire to Dogget who giggles so much the two men almost collapse in hysterics.

Masson looks blank, but Rupert has an inkling of what has passed.

'Let me guess, Dogget. I bet your guide wants to thank Francis very much for giving him his share.'

'Oh, it's much more than that,' says Dogget. 'He says that it would be his pleasure to give you his oldest wife, as it would allow him scope for one more wife – a younger one!'

At this, even the dour Scotsman laughs, raising his mug to the guide in salute. 'Tell him that's very kind – but on this occasion, I'll respectfully decline.'

Two days' later, Dogget suddenly stands up in his stirrups, gives the signal to halt and waves the other men to come and join him.

'Look.' He points at the horizon. 'The ocean. A few more days and we'll be in soft beds again.'

They start the steady descent and before long can see the Atlantic swells breaking on the beaches in the far distance. The going gets steeper, and the party are making a tricky descent along the path of a stream when the guide pulls at Dogget's sleeve, pointing to a small side track.

'This must be the place he mentioned.'

The guide speaks and points excitedly.

Dogget translates. 'He says that, if we go but fifteen minutes on foot, he can take us to a small plateau where he has seen the flowers of beauty he described.'

The men dismount, leaving the factotum to look after the horses whilst they trek off, following the guide. Fifteen minutes turns into nearly thirty. The track is quite tortuous, but just as the men are starting to get frustrated, they round a corner to discover a small plateau hanging off the mountainside, the remnant of ancient erosion.

The guide opens his arms in a gesture of welcome, whilst the three others look, open-jawed, at the vista before them. The plateau is covered in plants of awesome shape and structure, growing to the height of a man. The leaves are evergreen and arranged in two ranks, making a fan-shaped crown. Standing above the foliage, at the tips of long stalks, there is a hard, beak-like sheath, perpendicular to the stem, from which a flower erupts with the appearance of a bird's head and beak. The flowers themselves consist of three brilliant orange sepals and three purplish-blue and white petals.

Rupert is first to break the reverie. 'They look just like birds of paradise.'

Masson is jolted back into reality. 'Really? I've never seen one. But with plants so wonderful, who needs birds? Have you actually seen one, Rupert?'

'No, but we have a painting of one that my father acquired from the widow of the artist Joseph Banks took with him on *Endeavour*.'

'Sidney Parkinson,' Dogget interjects. 'I never met him – he died before he made Cape Town. Mr Banks told me he was a good man and a good artist.'

Rupert looks astounded. 'You have met Mr Banks?'

'Of course, when he docked at Cape Town on his way back to England.'

Rupert looks even more astounded. 'You never mentioned it.'

'You never asked. Anyway, I did him some small service here, and he said, should I ever get to England, I should call on him as he could always find use for a resourceful man.'

Rupert stares at him. Dogget smiles. 'By the way, I've also seen several real birds of paradise. Sailors brought them back from Java and the Australias in cages, and they were not uncommon in the Cape Verde islands. These flowers indeed do them justice. Although the flowers are quieter!'

Masson strides into the middle of the flowers. 'Birds aside, I'm sure we all wish Mr Banks was here to share this with us, but he is not. However, I do think we have found a flower worthy of our queen, or any queen for that matter. We must make camp here, or nearby.'

Dogget points down the hill to where the stream they have been following slows its course and meanders across a meadow.

'Good grass there for the horses and an easy enough walk for us back up to here.' He tells the guide to take the horses and the cart to the meadow and set up camp. Meanwhile, the botanists are in raptures over their find.

Rupert examines several flower heads. 'Francis, do you think these are seasonal? Or in this pleasant warm and moist climate, do you think they come into flower year-round? There seem to be flowers at all stages.'

Masson is equally focused on the ones that are in bloom and the ones that are not. 'I imagine, Rupert, you are considering what the chances are of presenting samples that are in flower to the King and Queen?'

'Indeed so.'

'Although it's only just coming to spring here, so if we could find specimens not yet in flower, pack them well and send them by ship with you... and perhaps find a way to control the light and warmth... You would be getting back to England for spring, and Her Majesty's birthday is in May.'

Rupert nods his enthusiasm. 'Perhaps we just take as many specimens as possible and hope it works out well enough that at least one flowering specimen survives to be presented on the Queen's birthday. In the meantime, I can sketch them so that, even if Her Majesty has to wait, Daisy can give her a painting of them in all their glory.'

The men pass the evening in high spirits. At sunrise the next day, they climb back up the hill and set to work – Dogget and Masson selecting specimens, Rupert taking measurements, picking complete flowers and leaves to press, and making pencil sketches.

Back in camp, as Masson starts to write up his notes, Rupert and Dogget set out with guns, the guide leading the way, to forage for the pot. The guide takes them into the undergrowth, moving silently – something Rupert, ten yards to the rear and the side, has had to get used to. Suddenly, both the guide and Dogget halt.

Rupert sees the guide's eyes look up to a low-hanging branch where an enormous snake is hanging down, just feet from the men's heads, its tongue flickering in and out of its mouth, taking in the scent of the two men frozen to the spot. The snake opens its jaws, exposing enormous, vicious fangs, and starts moving its head to and fro, ready to strike.

Far enough from the snake to be out of danger, Rupert slowly and silently lifts his gun to his shoulder, whispering *sotto voce* 'on three, dive'. Dogget in turn whispers to the guide. The snake, reacting to the sound, coils back its head.

'One, two, three, DIVE!' Rupert times it perfectly. As the two men hit the dirt, the snake strikes, Rupert pulls the trigger, the gun fires and the snake's head is blown to smithereens. The body slowly unwinds from the branch and falls to the ground in a heap as its intended victims scurry out of the way.

The guide talks excitedly to Dogget who turns to Rupert and smiles. 'He says there's food enough in the creature to get us to Cape Town.'

Rupert turns his nose up. Dogget picks up a large part of the beast and displays it. 'They do say what doesn't kill you makes you stronger!'

Rupert shakes his head and reloads his gun.

The guide winds the snake's torso round his body and walks back towards camp. Dogget gestures for Rupert to lead the way out of the bush. As Rupert walks past, Dogget takes him by the arm. 'Good shooting!'

'With a father in the army, I grew up around guns – although admittedly, he was in the artillery so most of them were cannons. Shooting is second nature to me. I have to say, though, that's my first snake. They're quite quick.'

Dogget looks at him steadily with his green eyes. 'Thank you. I owe you one.'

Rupert returns the gaze equally steadily. 'Lucky I'm not ophidiophobic. Let's go and find a few sand partridge for dinner, shall we?'

A few days later, with Cape Town on the horizon, Masson sends O'Flynn ahead to find out whether any vessels en route to England might be in port and, if so, to enquire about passage for Rupert and the specimen plants for the Queen.

Having made good speed, O'Flynn returns just over a day later.

'I bring good news, gentlemen. There is a merchantman in port waiting for some broken spars to be repaired. Being a businessman, the captain took the opportunity to sell some of the goods he was carrying whilst his ship was laid up, and so he has space in the hold and a spare cabin.'

Masson is delighted by the news. 'Have you secured the space, Mr O'Flynn – we wouldn't want him to fill his hold with something else.'

Dogget confirms he has with a nod.

Masson claps him on the shoulder. 'Well done, man. Now, Rupert'—he points to the plants in the back of the wagon—'do you think you'll be able to take care of them by yourself?'

Rupert looks concerned. 'A captain and crew I don't know, a voyage I have never done before, precious cargo for the Queen of the realm... To be honest, Francis, it makes me quite trepidatious. Anything could happen.'

Masson muses on this and strokes his chin.

Dogget is bursting to speak. 'Let me go with you!' he exclaims, almost shouting. 'Mr Masson'—he has never got used to calling the older man Francis—'you will be staying here on the Cape for another year at least – let me offer you my house to stay in, and send me away to England with Rupert.' He looks to his friend. 'That is if you don't mind having me – the cabin has room for two hammocks, and I know the voyage as far as the Verde archipelago very well.'

The other two look thoughtful. Dogget continues,

'Look, if push comes to shove, I'm a good man in a crisis.'

Rupert purses his lips thoughtfully. 'I'm the one who shot the snake.'

Dogget looks slightly down his nose. 'I'm the one that convinced you it was good eating!'

'An acquired taste, but yes, I seem to have acquired it – although I'm not expecting to encounter another such creature in the glasshouses at Kew Gardens and thereupon present it to Her Majesty's chef!'

Masson decides enough is enough. 'Gentlemen, let's stop the banter. Rupert, are you prepared to have Mr O'Flynn as company for the voyage, and vouch for him when you get to England?'

Rupert nods, and Masson turns to Dogget. 'Mr O'Flynn, are you happy to be charged with the responsibility of helping Mr Fitzgerald execute his duty to His Majesty King George in ensuring safe passage of certain specimens to Kew Gardens?'

Dogget nods his agreement. Rupert holds out his hand, and the two shake, grinning like schoolboys. Dogget breaks off first. 'This is wonderful news, gentlemen. I think we still have a bottle of rum or two left!' He turns and strolls off towards the wagon.

Masson winks at Rupert. 'Well, it's always good when a plan works out. You don't think we've taken advantage of him, do you?'

Rupert looks conspiratorial. 'Not at all. Better than we could have planned – as you have a decent house into the bargain.'

Masson smiles slowly. 'Yes, indeed. That will help Mr Bank's budget go further.'

'Spoken like a true Scotsman, Francis. Let's have a drink.'

As Rupert turns away, Masson adds a codicil to himself under his breath. 'Och, there's not going to be any sort of crisis that requires O'Flynn anyway.'

THE CHRISTMAS TREE

A t Kew, it is the depths of winter, the trees in the great garden standing like grey sticks against a grey sky. Out of doors, nature is sleeping, whilst in the great glasshouses, fires are lit to stop the plants becoming frostbitten.

As Daisy comes down to the kitchen in the pale early-morning light, Kate is poking life into the stove. 'Brrrr, Kate, these cold mornings are bad enough for me. They must be worse still for someone born in the colonies.'

Kate looks round. 'Not at all, miss – I love these mornings when you can see your breath hang in the air and the shapes the frost makes on the windowpane.'

'Yes, like ferns. I wonder what the botanists make of them.'

Kate makes tea. 'It's a shame Mr Fitzgerald isn't here to give his opinion. Do you miss him, miss?'

Daisy sips her tea and thinks about it. 'A little. Well, probably most days. At least he's in the warm weather.'

'The fact is it's much easier to keep warm in a cold climate than it is to keep cool in a hot one.'

'That's very wise, Kate. I do wonder how Mr Masson

and Mr Fitzgerald fared as they crossed the equator. Hopefully, they are somewhere with a sea breeze to cool them.'

With shorter days and the plants hibernating, Daisy spends some of her time painting seeds and fruits, but mostly, she is keeping up the Queen's painting lessons. Her boots leave footprints in the snow on the path between her studio and the Queen's cottage, visiting daily as the Queen and the countess both enjoy her company so.

One such afternoon, as a maid lights candles that reflect off the mirrors adorning the parlour walls, the Queen remarks that they should stop worrying about the enduring gloom as it will soon be the shortest day and the longest night.

Daisy puts down her brush. 'I've often wondered about that, Ma'am.'

The Queen raises an enquiring eyebrow. 'Wondered about what, dear?'

'I've always thought it's a bit of a conundrum, Ma'am. You see, the question is do we have two shortest days either side of a longest night or do we have two longest nights either side of one shortest day? And how does the earth know it is to turn around and come back towards the sun and summer?'

The countess coughs politely. 'Is that a question that ladies really need to concern themselves with?'

'I suppose not, milady. Perhaps it's a question I should address to Mr Banks.'

The Queen looks relieved. 'Quite so, but I have a question for *you*, Daisy.'

Daisy looks expectant, and the Queen continues. 'How are you keeping Christmas, my dear?'

'Quietly, Ma'am, I suppose. I have just myself to think of – I am letting my maid go to spend Christmas with her husband.'

The countess looks slightly disapproving. 'The black girl?'

'Yes, your ladyship. She is quite educated – her father was a preacher, she knows her bible and she reads well. On the feast of Christ's birth, it seems only Christian.' Daisy shrugs and smiles sweetly, as if it is the most natural thing to do.

The Queen looks a little resigned, as if humouring one of her children. 'Anyway, I command *you* to come and join us all on Christmas Eve when we light the candles on the tree in Kew Palace.'

Daisy looks wide-eyed. 'Tree, Ma'am?'

'Indeed, a tradition from my home in Germany. We light candles on a fir tree that we bring in from the garden, sing carols and make gifts to you all from His Majesty and myself.'

The countess looks excited. 'It is very pretty. Music and lights and hot punch – there is nothing more festive in this gloom of winter.'

The Queen claps her hands. 'Mr Banks comes, Mr Brown and his son will be there.' She turns to the countess, and tips her head. 'Madeleine, make a note to invite Meinheer Van der Humm too – I understand he has recently become a neighbour.' She smiles knowingly at Daisy.

Christmas Eve sees Daisy making her way towards Kew Palace, her footsteps crunching through a crisp frost. Servants in their finest livery are greeting visitors. The big entrance hall has a roaring fire and is lit by candles that reflect from the ceiling-high mirrors. A huge tree festooned with smaller candles stretches towards the ceiling.

Daisy hands her coat to a footman, walks in and crosses to near the fire, where she joins Banks, Van der Humm, Capability Brown and Brown's son Lance, chatting merrily. Banks makes space in the circle for her. 'Good evening, Daisy. Have you ever seen the like?'

Daisy looks carefully at the tree. 'It's quite beautiful, sir. But I do hope the tree doesn't catch fire.'

There is music, drinks and much good humour. The crowd parts slightly, people bow, and the King and Queen come into view, arm-in-arm.

Banks whispers in Daisy's ear. 'The King can be quite forgetful and erratic sometimes – he may not recognise you.'

The royal couple stop in front of Daisy's party who bow low.

The King regards them with an amused twinkle in his eye. 'Ah ha – the garden party,' he announces and looks around as people laugh.

The Queen takes his arm and beckons Daisy forwards.

'Your Majesty, this is Miss Salter who did the fine impressions of Meinheer Van der Humm's tulip planting and Mr Brown's new Hollow Walk. Remember, we did the planting together some time ago?'

Daisy makes her deepest curtsey, and the King holds out his hand for her to rise. 'Ah yes, your 'lady in painting'. Well, Miss Salter, the Queen's painting has certainly improved under your tutelage.'

Daisy blushes. 'Your Majesty, the Queen has a great talent for both painting and botany.'

The King smiles broadly. 'And you, Miss Salter, I see you have as good an eye for diplomacy as for pigments. Perhaps I should introduce you to young Mr Pitt. You might be able to teach him a thing or two.'

Daisy looks a bit bemused but the crowd chuckles.

The royal couple move on, and bonhomie is all around. A little later, the guests gather around the tree and sing along as the musicians play carols. Daisy joins in; she has a clear, sweet voice. Van der Humm moves to her side and hums along in a pleasant baritone.

'Meinheer, you know the tunes, but you do not know the words?'

'A lot of the tunes are familiar to me, but in my country the words are different.'

The orchestra starts the introduction to a new carol. Daisy recognises it. 'Meinheer, how is your Latin?'

In response, Van der Humm starts singing, '*In dulce jubilo...*'

Smiling, Daisy sings along with him and looks in amazement as the Queen moves over to join them. When they finish, people clap and the Queen turns to Daisy. 'The words may be in Latin, my dear, but it is a carol from my own country. And one of my favourites. That and the story of King Wenceslas who, family history suggests, was a distant relative of mine.'

'It is one of my favourites too, Your Majesty. The story of a king giving alms to a peasant is an inspiration for us all.'

By the tree, the King claps his hands. 'It is time for the Christmas presents.' The Queen joins him by a large pile of packages. A steward calls out names, and people move forwards to be given gifts.

When Daisy's turn comes, the Queen hands her a small, wrapped package.

Daisy feels her cheeks colour. 'Thank you, Your Majesty.'

'Daisy, my life has been so much more pleasant, not to say enlightened, since you came to Kew. Merry Christmas, my dear, but you mustn't open your gift until midnight.'

'Merry Christmas, Ma'am. My life has been so different since coming here too, and it has been quite wonderful to experience Your Majesty's kindness.'

The two women smile, at ease with each other. Daisy moves away, and Van der Humm, in close attendance, receives his gift next.

Quite soon, people begin departing, and Daisy, holding a lantern, walks out of the door and starts along the path home. As she turns a corner, a figure steps out of the shadows – it is Lance Brown. Feeling unsettled, Daisy lengthens her stride, but Brown keeps pace.

'Hello there, Daisy. May I walk you home?'

Daisy backs away and holds the lantern high so that she can see his face. 'Thank you, but I know the way and I am perfectly capable.'

The man steps in front of Daisy and puts his hands on her arms. 'How about a little festive kiss then?'

Daisy tries to pull away. 'How dare you! Mr Brown! Have you been drinking?'

Brown thinks for a moment. 'Well, perhaps one or two. Oh, hang on, I get it, you've never been kissed before, have you? Well, Christmas is the perfect time to start!'

He pulls Daisy close; she struggles and tries to kick his shins, but he has the strength of a man used to manual labour and she is firmly trapped. He is about to kiss her when she hears footsteps on the gravel and a loud voice.

'Stop that! Unhand her now!' It is Van der Humm, who pulls Lance from Daisy and drags him away, speaking to Daisy over his shoulder. 'Miss Salter, stay there, I'll deal with him and be back.'

Van der Humm drags Lance round the corner, makes a fist with his right hand and punches it hard into his left palm three times with a resounding slapping noise. Daisy hears Brown's voice.

'Hey, stop it, leave me alone. That hurts. It was only a bit of fun with a silly girl!'

'That "silly girl" is far too good for the likes of you.' Van der Humm's voice splits the night as he punches his palm one last time. Take that for your insolence.' He takes a purse from his pocket and gives it to Brown who winks. 'Now clear off, and if I catch you near Miss Salter again, you will get much worse than a slight beating.'

Waiting with her heart racing, Daisy can hear footsteps running away. Van der Humm returns, and she rushes into his arms. 'Meinheer, meinheer, thank you. Thank you so much.'

Van der Humm comforts Daisy, her head pressed against his fur-trimmed coat, and smiles over her shoulder. He is smiling at Lance who has returned to peer around the corner of the building waving the purse of money. Van der Humm offers Daisy his arm. 'Come now, let me see you to your door.'

Their footsteps crunch along the gravel path, the way lit by Daisy's lantern and the glow of the moon. Eventually, they stand face-to-face in the porch of Daisy's cottage.

'Meinheer, it has been a strange evening. I do not know if it is the excitement of being rescued by you, or the wine – but I feel quite intoxicated.'

Van der Humm stares deeply into her eyes. 'I am pleased I was there to rescue you. I know you are alone with no maid, so I will not presume to come in. But I do have a present to give you.' He hands her a package.

Daisy looks up, her face flushed, her eyes shining. 'Thank you, meinheer. This is most kind.'

'Unexpected?'

'I would not want to expect anything, meinheer.' She lowers her voice. 'There is one thing Brown said that did make me think.'

Van der Humm, who by now has his hands on her arms, pushes her slightly away to look at her better. 'What was that?'

Daisy bites her lip. 'He said it's obvious that I've never been kissed... but that Christmas is the perfect time to start.'

Van der Humm leans forwards, puts his hand under her chin, lifts her mouth to his and kisses her tenderly but briefly.

'Good night, Miss Salter.'

Daisy put her hand to his cheek. 'Call me Daisy.'

Merry Christmas, Daisy. Call me Johannes.'

'Merry Christmas... Johannes.'

Van der Humm brushes his lips against hers, and she looks him in the eye. 'Goodnight, Daisy, sleep well.' With a gentle squeeze of her arm, he turns and leaves.

Inside her cottage, she lights the candles and stokes the fire in the grate. Daisy takes a seat at the table with her presents in front of her. In the distance, she hears Kew's clock strike midnight. She picks up one present in each hand and weighs them up, deciding which to open first. She settles on the Queen's gift, lavishly wrapped, and pulls the paper apart to reveal a painting of a rose in a silver frame – it is inscribed 'To my English rose' and initialled CvMS. Daisy looks at it appraisingly for a few seconds before nodding and putting it down.

Then she picks up Van der Humm's present. The discreetly elegant package contains a mixture of fine-haired paintbrushes tied with red velvet ribbon, and a note. Daisy takes the ribbon and ties it into her hair. Then she opens and reads the note, which says 'These are from the same Amsterdam brush-maker as patronised by Meinheer Van Rijn.'

Daisy turns to the portrait of her father on the wall. 'Papa,' she whispers, 'I miss you, and I miss Sudbury. But I'm starting to feel at home here.' She retires to bed, laying the brushes given to her by Van der Humm on the pillow next to her, the red velvet ribbon still in her hair.

QUEEN'S COUNSEL

Two days later, at the Queen's painting lesson, Daisy seems agitated, seeking an opportunity to speak. The Queen looks up from her work.

'Well, girl, what is it?'

'Ma'am, I wanted to thank you for my gift. It was nicely done.'

The Queen looks back to her work. 'I'm glad you like it. But you seem unsettled. Is something wrong?'

Daisy hesitates, her eyes starting to tear up. 'Ma'am, on Christmas Eve, a young man tried to take advantage of me.'

The Queen looks sympathetic but unsurprised. 'Men always take advantage of women – that is their nature. Especially women your age without a husband. A woman needs a man's protection.'

'Majesty, are you and the King in love and happily married?'

'Why, Daisy, yes we are. He even calls me Mrs King! Of course, not all kings and queens are in love. Most marry for duty. We are lucky.'

Daisy looks rather tortured. 'Majesty. I think I may have fallen in love.'

The Queen smiles fondly. 'Is it Meinheer Van der Humm? He has nice manners, is easy on the eye, is tall and strong, and as I believe he buys you perfume from Floris, he has good taste and a generous disposition – what is not to like?

'I'm so scared.'

The Queen reaches over and takes her by the hand. 'Never be frightened of love. Every woman needs to marry. If it is true love, everything will work out as planned. Love always finds a way.'

Daisy gives her a beseeching look. 'I feel so unprepared.'

'But you have time, and you must make time to take time. Time is everything. Sometimes love makes time go faster and sometimes slows it down. When things go wrong, it is always later than we think. If things go right, it is sooner than we imagine.'

The Queen stands, walks to the window and looks out. 'Whether it's an early spring or a late winter, flowers always bloom – all we need is patience. Nature knows her course, and it is best to follow it. Especially with men, who cannot be hurried because they cannot think quickly enough to see the obvious.'

Daisy walks to the window and joins her. 'Majesty, you know so very much – I feel I know so little.'

The Queen waves a dismissive hand. 'You are just at the start. After eight children, and I imagine more to come, nature has taught me that repetition is a virtue. Women know that; men need to learn it.'

That same night finds Van der Humm sitting in front of a large fire across a table from de Vries in the private room of an inn. As ever, he has been rowed here under cover of darkness.

He raises his glass in salute. 'Happy Christmas, meinheer.'

The older man follows suit. '*Fijne kerst*, Johannes. How was your gift received by the girl?'

'Very well. It was a clever idea of yours.'

De Vries accepts the compliment with a nod. 'And the romance?'

'We have exchanged kisses.'

De Vries lifts an enquiring eyebrow. 'Surely not too onerous a task?'

Van der Humm shrugs. 'She is a little… shall we say, thin of lip for my taste.'

'Of course, I know your preferences. But you should learn to enjoy what she has to offer. It is time for you to propose marriage to this woman.'

Van der Humm says nothing for a moment, trying to see what is in the eyes of his compatriot – but the candles reflecting on his spectacles make it impossible. 'Is that really necessary?'

'Johannes – think clearly. Marriage to this girl will position you only one conversation away from the Queen. Women gossip and all information is good information. And you could plant our questions in her mind.'

Van der Humm drains his glass and refills it. 'It is a lot to ask.'

De Vries polishes his spectacles, and the two sit in

silence for a few moments, Van der Humm staring into the fire.

'You may have heard the rumour yourself, Johannes, but people are saying the King is more than a little mad. We would like to know more about that – and who might be running the country. You can trust me to see to it that you will be wealthy, and the girl has an income that would naturally become yours.'

Van der Humm squirms in his chair. 'But married to the same woman for life – it's a lot to take.'

De Vries replenishes both glasses again. 'Even a roué like you has to grow up sometime. Besides, you will have your "black tulip" experiment for solace. You can go into business with that dreadful brother-in-law of hers, and who knows, Banks may discover a new plant so exciting that it could spark another tulip fever. If you are positioned to know about such a thing early on, we and our countrymen will be well placed to corner the market!'

Van der Humm looks unconvinced. De Vries raises a toast. 'To marriage!' Resignedly, Van der Humm reaches across and chinks glasses. As the younger man goes to leave, de Vries calls him back.

'One more thing, Johannes. Don't be too visible at Kew for a few weeks – she will wonder where you are, and absence always helps the heart grow fonder.'

Van der Humm turns from the door. 'I assume you are a married man then, meinheer, to know such things?'

De Vries takes a pull on his drink and smiles slowly. 'Married? Me? There has never been any purpose in me being married – marriage is for men of ambition... like you.'

Van der Humm steps back to the table, takes a pull on his drink and says nothing.

'Anyway, Johannes, I have made your suit even easier. We have heard word from the Cape that your... shall we say, competitor in love, Mr Fitzgerald, returns to England with a mysterious cargo that we can only assume is valuable.'

Van der Humm coughs and spits onto the sawdust floor.

De Vries regards him critically. 'I do hope that you do not display such manners at Kew.' He refills his glass. 'Anyway, after his ship has called at Cadiz, I have arranged that he will never return home – and we will intercept the cargo. At the appropriate time, you can inform Miss Salter you are sure he has perished off the coast of France.'

The candles glint in Van der Humm's eyes as his mouth forms a slow, cruel smile, and he raises his glass to salute his mentor.

THE LONG NINE

Visiting Cadiz was always on the cards; Rupert and Dogget have known from the outset that the captain has business there. Regardless, it made sense because although the plants are thriving, like the vessel in general, they were in need of fresh water, and Rupert was keen to visit the medicinal plants in the famous botanical gardens.

All went well in Cadiz, but the trouble started within forty-eight hours of leaving port for England. By the time the sun rose the following morning, half of the crew were dead. The rest look to be at death's door.

'That's the captain gone now,' Rupert says resignedly, as he and Dogget, stripped to the waist in the heat of the day, consign his body to a watery grave. 'This makes life somewhat less certain.'

The darker-skinned man turns to his red-haired companion. 'Remember when I pulled you out of that waterfront inn because I didn't like the smell of the food?'

Rupert nods.

'But the crew ignored me and filled their bellies, making the most of their last meal ashore before England?'

Rupert nods again.

'It's turned out to be their last meal ever.' Dogget looks

grim. 'Food poisoning. I've seen it before. What worries me now is what if it was deliberate? Somewhere in our wake'—he points over the aft of the ship—'there could be a privateer waiting for us all to die, so they can come alongside and capture the ship. I witnessed the same strategy on the triangular trade – pirates picking up vessels and cargo for nothing.'

Rupert grasps him by the forearm. 'Well, it's either all doom and gloom, or we can embrace it as an adventure. Neither you nor I ate that food, we still have five of the crew hanging on to life by the skin of their teeth, and I for one am not in the business of surrender.'

'And I've never run from a fight, and—'

'You have the scars to prove it!' Rupert finishes his sentence. 'If I'm not mistaken, you know how to sail this vessel blindfolded. Do you also know how we might save at least some of the crew?'

'We took on a cargo of oranges in Cadiz. In my experience, oranges have some quite strong medicinal powers. If we can get what's left of the crew to eat them, or drink the juice, they may have a chance.'

Rupert salutes his friend. 'Right, leave that to me! Now whilst you're the sort of chap who's never run from a fight...'

Dogget nods, so Rupert continues. 'Might I suggest we don't go looking for one?'

'Never have yet. I can steer the ship, and I can make the most of the wind, but the question is whether, for the next twenty-four to forty-eight hours, you can learn how to trim the sails?'

 180

'Tell me what I need to do, and at least I can die trying.'

Rupert manages to get four of the crew to eat some oranges, but for one poor soul, he was too late. They consign the body to the waves, and then Rupert does what he can to hoist and trim sails whilst Dogget takes the wheel. Even so, come nightfall, it is apparent they have slowed down dramatically.

Taking it in turns at the wheel overnight, they make what progress they can, but as the watch changes at sunrise, Dogget looks astern. 'As I feared, Rupert, we're being pursued.' He points to the horizon, and one glance shows they are being chased by a vessel flying the full complement of canvas, visibly closing the distance.

Rupert is at the wheel when Dogget comes up from below decks having visited the crew. 'They survived the night, but they're still too weak to be of any use. Do you have any ideas as to how we get out of this?'

Rupert looks pensive for a moment then smiles. 'Yes, we turn and fight – if we're going to go down, then I say we go down all guns blazing!'

Dogget stares at him in disbelief. 'Are you mad? We don't even have a gun!'

'That's where you're wrong, captain.' Rupert claps him on the shoulder. 'There's a long nine tucked away in the hold at the front.' He sees Dogget's bemused look. 'Do you know what a long nine is, and why we're lucky to have one?'

With a gesture that suggests Rupert is barking mad, Dogget shakes his head.

'A long nine has a longer barrel than most cannons –

and it's specifically used as what's called a bow chaser or a stern chaser because it's too big to be mounted transversely between decks.'

'So why are we lucky to have one?' Dogget checks astern and notes their pursuers are closer than ever.

'Because of its longer barrel it has a longer range and it's more accurate, of course! That chasing vessel won't expect us to defend ourselves from a distance, so we'll have the element of surprise.'

'Well, that may be obvious to you, but it means nothing to me, not to mention we know nothing about firing a cannon.'

Rupert stands upright and puffs out his chest. 'Speak for yourself, O'Flynn. I am the son of the ex-commander of His Majesty's Artillery and Ordnance. I spent my childhood with my father, amongst guns and cannons.'

Dogget looks doubtful. 'Did you ever fire one?'

'Certainly not, dirty sort of job. But I know how they work, and I've aimed them, trained them and ranged them. Putting the fire in the hole is the easy bit.'

'I'm not convinced, but you think we should put this long nine piece on the stern then?'

'Ah, how easy is it to turn the ship around?'

'You want to fight them face-to-face?'

'Yes, having checked the powder locker, we only have enough for ten shots – of course I expect to hit them much quicker than that, but I'd like to hit them up close. The long nine has a range of about a mile, but I'd prefer to have a pot at them from about a thousand yards. If we could turn around, drop most of the sails and sit still on the water, I could use the swell to help with the elevation and have more chance of doing damage.'

Dogget strokes a beard grown fuller and longer during the voyage. 'If we did that, they might think we were going to surrender. What will you aim for? A nine-pound cannonball won't exactly sink her.'

'Actually, I thought I'd hit her twice. First, let's take her mast down, then we'll put a shot through her bow near the waterline. If she starts shipping water, she'll have no choice but to slow down.'

'I have to say I admire your confidence. But I think you're mad. Then again, I have no better plan, so very well.'

At that moment, two of the crew, looking frail, emerge from below decks. One is an old salt, the other no more than a teenager. The older one speaks. 'We're not in the best shape, sir, but we've seen the ship chasing us astern, and we're reporting for duty.'

Dogget looks delighted and points to the speaker. 'You take the wheel. Keep her on a steady course whilst we get the cannon from below decks. The youngster can help us bring up powder and shot. When we're set, we'll slowly go about and look like a sitting duck.'

'A duck with a very large quack,' adds Rupert.

Within an hour, the cannon is mounted in the bow and roped for recoil. The two crew members are recovering some strength – enough to be of assistance. Rupert designates them as the firing party, showing them how to load and prepare the weapon. The vessel is turned around to face the assailant rapidly closing in.

To Dogget's bemusement, Rupert is fiddling around with the ship's sextant.

'The thing is, Mr O'Flynn, gunnery is mostly about the science of trigonometry – the elevation required is a question of distance. On the firing ranges of his regiment, my father had the ground marked at hundred-yard intervals. Up to a thousand yards, my feel for distance is quite exact. It comes in very useful when you are planning a garden.'

'I will take your word for it, Mr Fitzgerald. Are they in range yet?'

'Not quite,' Rupert responds calmly. 'Where's the spyglass, Dogget? My first shot may not be entirely accurate, and I'll need you to see where it falls. I estimate the fuse will burn for three seconds, and I have timed the rise and fall of the swell. We will fire at the top of the swell, and you will spot for us please.'

Ten suspenseful minutes pass before Rupert is ready. He makes one last check of the sextant. 'If my calculations are correct, the elevation and distance will be perfect. We light the fuse the moment we are at the top of the swell.'

He squints along the length of the cannon, lining it up on the chasing vessel. 'Let us have a rehearsal, so don't fire now, but we will pretend to fire on my count of three.' He waits until the swell is almost at the top and counts one, two, three.

The gun crew pretend to fire. Dogget, following the pursuers through the telescope, calls 'Don't be too long, Rupert – now we have turned and halted, they are closing rapidly.'

'Let's waste no more time then. This time it's for real.'

The fuse fizzles as the bow rises, Rupert counts to three and, at the top of the arc, there is an almighty explosion accompanied by a billow of smoke. As it blows away, Dogget raises the telescope to his eye.

'My God, Rupert! I don't believe it! You've taken the mainmast down with your first shot.' He is grinning ear-to-ear. 'Must be beginner's luck!'

'Let's see if I can prove it wasn't any such thing.' Rupert is grinning too and instructs the men to reload.

Dogget puts out his hand to stop them. 'No, they cannot catch us now, and I have seen enough sailors perish at sea. There is no need to sink them.' He turns to the crew. 'Get aloft, you men – let's put on what canvas we can; we'll go about and make a beat for home.'

As the men get about their business, he shakes Rupert by the hand. 'Beginner's luck or not, I salute you. Thank you. The last thing I had hoped for was to die in the middle of the Atlantic at the hands of pirates.'

Rupert meets his steady gaze. 'Let me assure you, it wasn't beginner's luck. To get the mast with the first ball was fortuitous, but without doubt, I would have had him. Trust me in this, and in other things once we make landfall in England.'

'I'm starting to think I might, *master gunner*, although we have to get through the Bay of Biscay first.'

The two smile and shake hands again.

GRAVE NEWS

It is mid-February at Kew. The days are getting noticeably longer and plants like the camellias, always precocious, are starting to show a renaissance of life. Snowdrops poke their noses above the ground and daffodil stalks start thrusting upwards.

Daisy is working intently in her studio when Van der Humm enters. It's the first time she has seen him since Christmas.

'Johannes! What a pleasant surprise.' She stands up, flustered, her hands playing with her hair. 'You have been absent from Kew for some weeks, since Christmas.' She blushes in memory of the kiss.

'Indeed, I have been back to my homeland on business. Having returned, I wanted to see you to tell you that I now have to travel to Liverpool to inspect a cargo from your brother. However, upon my return I would hope to speak with you?'

Daisy looks at him in a puzzled fashion. 'Of course, meinheer. But will you not stay and take tea?'

'Thank you, but sadly, I must make haste.' He walks over, takes her hand, raises it to his lips and kisses it. 'I will return within ten days or so.'

Daisy holds his hand a moment longer. 'Take care, meinheer. I will look forward to your safe return.'

Van der Humm kisses her hand again and lets his fingertips linger over hers in a caress before taking his own hand away. 'I will look forward to that too.'

Daisy smiles as he turns and goes, then her face suddenly drops, uncertain about her emotions for him.

Two weeks later, Daisy and Banks are examining specimens in one of the glasshouses when Van der Humm, looking grave, enters and approaches them.

Banks extends his hand in greeting then looks at the Dutchman's face and withdraws it. 'Meinheer – you look as if you have seen a ghost.'

Van der Humm looks from one to the other solemnly. He lifts his heavy satchel off his shoulder, pulls out a chair and sits down heavily. When he looks back up at Daisy, his eyes are sorrowful. 'If only it was that, sir. I am afraid I am the bringer of sad news. In Liverpool, I met a ship's captain of my acquaintance who, just returned from south of the equator, told me that Mr Masson's and Mr Fitzgerald's ship was sunk in a storm and that all on board perished.'

Daisy slumps onto a nearby bench, looking distraught and wringing her hands. 'No, meinheer! That cannot be. How can you be sure?'

Van der Humm crosses to sit beside her. 'Daisy, Biscay is one of the most notorious stretches of water between here and the Cape of Africa. The storms are fierce and shipwrecks far too common.'

Banks has been pacing, stroking his chin. 'Yet, meinheer, they must have crossed Biscay many months ago.'

Van der Humm, thinking on his feet, shrugs his shoulders. 'I understand, Mr Banks, that Fitzgerald was on a return journey. Some of my countrymen sailing out of Bordeaux found not only ship's wreckage after a fearful storm, but boxes marked with the word "Specimens: Handle with care", addressed to Kew Gardens.'

Banks looks serious. 'This is grave news indeed. Do you know the whereabouts, meinheer?'

'Somewhere off the north coast of Iberia, to the south of Biscay.'

'Do others know?'

'I am, I think, the first hereabouts.'

Daisy recovers enough to speak. 'But how, sir, do you *know* Mr Fitzgerald was on board?'

'The Dutch consul in the Cape Verde islands has a record of a vessel carrying Mr Fitzgerald putting in for water and provisions – he was sailing on a northward heading.'

Banks bustles out, frowning. Van der Humm puts his arms around Daisy who sobs into his chest.

'Did you love Mr Fitzgerald, Daisy?'

Daisy pushes herself away, dries her eyes and regards him keenly, suddenly aware that she must be careful what she says. 'No. No, of course I didn't love him. But he was my friend.'

'Then he is a great loss. But time will heal the pain, and perhaps I may visit you more often and help distract you from your grief?'

Daisy takes a small handkerchief out of one of her voluminous painting pockets, blows her nose, tidies her hair and smooths her dress before replying. 'Thank you, Johannes, that would be most kind. I would welcome your visits.'

Later that afternoon, Daisy is ushered into the Queen's parlour to find the countess sitting on the floor, in tears, head resting on the Queen's lap.

'Ma'am. You have heard about Rupert's ship?'

The Queen pats the countess' head and puts a finger to her lips in a shush gesture, then points to the countess. 'You may have lost a friend, my dear, but the countess has lost a son.'

Daisy's face goes through a range of emotions, and she rushes over to the countess, kneels on the floor and puts her arms around her. 'I am so very sorry, your ladyship. I did not know he was your son. I was very fond of him, and he was very kind to me.'

The countess looks up, red-eyed. 'He was a shy, kind and generous boy who has been taken far too soon. He was so very fond of you too. He talked about you a lot, and he talked about you often. Best you forget him now.'

The conversation is interrupted by a knock on the door. A footman enters. 'The Earl of Clonmel, Your Majesty.'

Clonmel bustles in looking businesslike. He bows to the Queen. 'Ma'am, I came as soon as I heard the news.' He then notices Daisy. 'Miss Salter, it seems somehow appropriate for you to be here to share our reported loss.'

Daisy is quick to grasp the nuance. '*Reported* loss, my lord?'

Clonmel has moved to comfort his wife. 'In my job, Miss Salter, you learn to fear for the worst yet hope for the best, and in my experience, it is six of one and half-a-dozen of the other. We will keep the faith for a while until we have definite confirmation. I have men who will check the facts. Remember what was left in Pandora's Box!'

'Yes, the last thing left was *hope*, my lord. I will do as you say and hope, then. And offer my prayers for his safe return.'

The countess reaches out and squeezes Daisy's hand. 'Let us hope you are as good at talking to the Almighty as you are at representing the beauties of nature He has sent us.'

The Queen catches Daisy's eye and nods her thanks. Daisy quietly leaves them to their grief and hurries back to her cottage. It is as if the weather has sensed the mood, and a shower brings unseasonal hail, which stings her skin so she arrives red-faced, darts inside out of the weather and closes the door firmly behind her. She stands there, back leaning against the frame.

Kate bustles up to her. 'Miss, this is an unexpected hour.' She proffers a towel and dabs at Daisy's cheeks. Then she realises that despite drying off the hail and rain, the cheeks remain wet.

'Why, miss, you're crying. Whatever is the matter?'

Daisy throws her arms around the comforting substance of the older woman and sobs raggedly into her shoulder. 'Oh Kate, it is Mr Fitzgerald. It's been said he is lost at sea.'

Kate hugs her, leads her into the parlour, sits her down and sets to making tea. 'I've stirred a good dollop of honey into your tea, miss. On the plantations, whenever anybody had a bad shock, they gave them cane sugar to suck on – sugar helps comfort bad news.'

'Thank you, Kate.' Daisy sips and sighs. 'I don't know what to think. I discovered this afternoon that Rupert was the son of the countess.'

'Yes, miss. The Viscount Minnella.'

Daisy looks at her, amazed. 'How did you know that?'

'Servants know a lot of things, miss. It helps us to look after the interests of our masters and mistresses, not to mention our own.'

Once again, Daisy sees her in a new light.

'The thing is, miss, we just don't talk about what we know. A well looked after servant is one of the best people in the world at keeping confidences.'

'Nothing even a little clandestine, Kate?'

'Certainly not, miss. Might I ask you, miss, if you were in love with him?'

Faced with the same question twice in one day, Daisy comes up with a slightly different answer.

'I'm not sure, Kate. I'm still so uncertain about men and love. I have had two men who have shown me much affection, and I feel affection for both in return.' She sighs deeply. 'Until now, I always thought I would have a choice

– not that I would have found that easy.'

'Miss, there is still so much time. You're not exactly an old maid yet.'

Kate smiles a serendipitous smile. After a few tense seconds, Daisy relaxes and smiles too.

SPRING SURPRISES

With no news of Rupert, Kew mourns the loss of a son and valued colleague, the world turns and Mother Nature displays her spring robes. The day soon comes when a party of nobility and gardeners alike assemble above the tulip field.

Van der Humm is waiting. The Queen and her entourage arrive, wearing blindfolds as Van der Humm has requested of them. Men help the party down from carriages and into line along the brow of the vantage point. Van der Humm counts to three, and the guests remove their blindfolds. 'The tulips are up. Spring is here!'

The Queen claps her hands in glee. 'They are beautiful, like glorious birds perched there. I particularly like the ones of different colours – the yellow and red ones remind me of the parrots in His Majesty's menagerie at Tower Hill.' She looks to Daisy. 'Perhaps you will take some and paint them for me, my dear?'

'It would be an honour, Ma'am.'

The Queen turns away, then turns back and beckons Daisy across to her. She leans forwards and whispers into Daisy's ear, 'But first take the most splendid and paint them for the countess – she needs something bright in her life.' She squeezes Daisy's arm.

The tulips look both magnificent and stunning, massive drifts of colours across the far slope, except for the paths that were left unplanted at Daisy's suggestion. Van der Humm makes an expansive and all-embracing gesture over the vista, and the Queen, marvelling at the riot of colour, leads her party down the hill.

Daisy, who has followed the entire progress of the tulips sprouting and coming into bloom, stands with Van der Humm. Since his return from Liverpool, she has adroitly avoided any serious conversation with him, taking care to always have another person present. Now they are alone for the first time, and with all the others distracted, marvelling at the tulips, he surreptitiously slips his hand into hers, all the while regarding the sight in front of him.

Daisy startles and goes to take her hand away. Then she regains her composure, leaving it where it is as she looks up at him and smiles. 'The flowers are beautiful, Johannes – you must be very proud.'

Turning towards her, he smiles back. 'There are many beautiful things here, today. Later, when this show is over'—he nods his head in the direction of the crowd—'may I come to you at your studio?'

Daisy swallows hard and looks down, knowing the moment is coming that may decide her future. She finds she can't look him in the eye but, turning away, manages to nod her agreement. Finally, she looks back at him. 'Yes, of course.'

Back in her studio, Daisy arranges the tulips she has picked in a blue and white Dutch vase. She is finding it hard to concentrate as she stands over her worktable fussing with her paintbrushes. The door opens, and Van der Humm enters. He crosses the room, places his hands lightly on her shoulders, turns her to face him and then holds her at arm's-length. Daisy's body stiffens slightly.

'Meinheer, I take it the tulips are left to fend for themselves?'

'For all their beauty and no matter how much I admire them, I do not think they are in need of my protection. But there is another flower, much more beautiful, that I admire even more, that I want to offer my protection to.'

Daisy colours and looks flustered. She closes her eyes tightly for a few seconds then opens them, looks straight at him and summons a smile to her face. 'Which flower might that be, Johannes?'

'It is you, Daisy.' He gets down on one knee. 'Would you consent to be my wife?'

Daisy looks down at him. 'Meinheer, you do me a great honour. But I have never been one to make a decision on impulse – can you give me a few days to think?'

Van der Humm stands up, taking both of Daisy's hands in his. 'Of course. Today is Thursday – I travel on business tomorrow. May I visit you on Sunday for an answer?'

Daisy smiles wanly, pleased for the reprieve. 'Come to my cottage at ten, before we go to church. My maid has been experimenting with making coffee – do you know, it doesn't taste too unpleasant at all with a dash of milk in it.'

Van der Humm raises his eyebrows. 'Be careful! If you offer a Dutchman good coffee, he will fall even more in love with you.' He moves to kiss her, but she backs away. Instead, he brushes the back of her hand with his lips.

'You have used the word *love,* meinheer. I think I need to consider that and ask my unpractised heart if it feels the same way.'

Van der Humm knows well enough not to push her too hard. 'To Sunday, might I come to church with you? It will, hopefully, be the first time of many!'

Again, she simply nods. Looking pleased with himself, Van der Humm turns on his heel and leaves.

Tormented by indecision, Daisy plays abstractedly with her brushes then sits down and puts her head in her hands, feeling in great need of advice.

As Kew's great clock sounds two o'clock in the afternoon, Daisy knocks on the door of the Queen's cottage. She is shown into the parlour where the Queen is singing a lullaby to her youngest baby. The Queen hands the baby to the wet nurse.

'Daisy? I wasn't expecting you until three. Have you painted the tulips already?'

Daisy shakes her head, looking at her shoes.

'Well, dear girl, what on earth is the matter?'

'Your Majesty... Ma'am, can I ask your counsel?'

The Queen sits and indicates for Daisy to do the same.

'Let me guess... meinheer has made you a proposal of marriage?'

'Well, yes. How did you know?'

'It was only a matter of time. What was your reply?'

'That I needed time to think about it.'

'Do you love him?'

'Ma'am, I am a scientist – what do scientists know about love?'

'But you are also a woman.'

'But why must I decide between the work I know I love and marrying a man I'm not sure I do? And *how* do I decide?'

'You are lucky to have the option. I had no part in deciding. I was a girl of seventeen who, six hours after meeting him, married a man my brother had chosen as my husband. You are much better informed, and you have options.'

Daisy looks at the Queen. 'Perhaps that is so, but you are in love with the King.'

'That came later. He was a nice boy; I was with child within two months, bore him an heir and he has cared for me all these years. Now he is my best friend, and I am his.'

Daisy looks at her blankly.

'Daisy, have you asked meinheer what sort of wife he expects you to be? He may welcome your connections at Kew – he is an ambitious man, and your friendships here may suit him.'

'Your Majesty, I had not thought of that. Is it a good or a bad thing?'

'It is simply a thing – in most marriages one or both sides look to gain. Take me – I gained a king, and the King gained a princess from a little-known Duchy in Germany whom he knew was of no political importance.' She smiles at the recollection. Daisy… ask him about the things that worry you. Men and women rarely communicate as well as they should. You are an honest and, I must say, intelligent and educated woman. It doesn't have to be your heart – use your head first.'

That evening, when she returns to her cottage for supper, there is a letter on the table. It is from her sister Fanny in Rutland. It has been a warm and testing day, and Daisy asks Kate to bring her a mug of cider, regarding the letter somewhat suspiciously.

'Are you not going to open it, miss?' Kate asks.

Daisy breaks the seal. 'I just hope it contains no more unhappy news.'

Kate is trying not to be nosy, busying herself bustling around the kitchen. Finally, Daisy finishes reading, lays the letter back on the table, breathes deeply and exhales, her shoulders drooping.

'Bad news, miss?'

'Not exactly, Kate, but Fanny once again failed to produce an heir for the title. Furthermore, it seems Hugo's brother Greville is rather pleased about it as Hugo is some years older than him. If Hugo dies, Greville will inherit everything.'

Kate touches Daisy on the shoulder. 'Life seems so

unfair to women, miss. Lady Fanny has given Lord Godolphin a fair few years of her life, two beautiful daughters and is a wonderful hostess.'

'Quite, Kate. And here am I faced with a decision to give my life to a man I still know so little about.'

'That would mean protection and security, miss.'

'Or it might mean the end to everything I hold so dear.'

Sunday dawns bright. Daisy, dressed for church, is sitting in front of a mirror whilst Kate pins up her hair.

'Cheer up, miss. It isn't the end of the world when a man comes to ask for your hand in marriage. Especially such a handsome one... and tall – there is something about a tall man.'

'Your Mr Gardner is not that tall!'

'He has a big heart, miss, and when it comes to hearts, every woman knows that size matters.'

'Yet I have no idea of the size of meinheer's heart. He has given me gifts, he has been kind to me, he has said pretty things, but how do I know what is really in his heart?' She looks beseechingly at Kate's reflection. 'Kate, what should I do?'

Kate puts down the comb. 'It was different for me, miss. My husband and I... well, we grew up together. I had plenty of chance to compare him with other boys, and he had plenty of chance to compare me with other girls. It made things easy because we spent more and more time together. When he asked me, I knew that anybody else would be second best, and I knew he felt the same.' She picks up some ribbon and starts weaving it through Daisy's hair.

'That's all very well for you, Kate. I have no comparisons.'

'Excuse me, miss, but there *was* one.'

Daisy regards her sharply.

'Mr Fitzgerald, miss.'

Daisy's shoulders drop. 'Yes, but he is not just lost to me, but to the world.'

'But it's still a comparison, miss. You can at least ask yourself whether, had Mr Fitzgerald also proposed, would you have preferred his hand to meinheer's?'

Daisy opens a drawer on her dressing table, takes out Rupert's painting of the daisy chain and smooths it on her lap. 'He did propose, Kate – after a fashion. At least I think that's what it was. He asked me to wait for him to return from the Cape.'

She hands the paper to Kate who scrutinises it carefully. 'Typical of a man, miss, slightly clumsy... but ever so sweet. And there is no doubting his intention, I would say the painter shows a distinct passion for daisies – just like Mr Gardner and his melons.'

'I fear, Kate, you have the right of it and that I was in the wrong. At least, had I told Mr Fitzgerald I would wait for him, I would not now be facing this quandary.'

'Best put Mr Fitzgerald from your mind, miss. He's not coming back now, so even if you might have preferred his suit...?' She looks in the mirror at Daisy.

Daisy's eyes slide away from the inquisitive regard. 'Perhaps I might, Kate. But as you say, best forget him.'

In the distance, the clock chimes the three-quarter-hour. Daisy clenches her fists. 'I have fifteen minutes, Kate. What will I say?'

'He will be expecting you to say yes. Most men are arrogant like that. You told me Her Majesty suggested you ask him about the longer-term intentions he has for you both. Ask him questions – being inquisitive always unsettles a man. Don't give yourself to him easily – if he doesn't convince you, there is still time to decline his suit. Compose yourself and put him to the test.'

'Thank you, Kate. I suppose there is only one question, really.'

Daisy sits composed on her sofa. There is a knock at the door. Kate enters and bobs a curtsey.

'Meinheer Van der Humm, miss.'

Daisy stands to greet him. Kate leaves and quietly closes the door. 'Meinheer, you are punctual. You have come for your answer?'

For once in his life, Van der Humm looks nervous. He just nods.

'Johannes, I need to ask you one very important question. If I agree to be your wife, do you propose to spirit me off to the depths of Amsterdam, which, as we know, smells of fish...'

Van der Humm raises a smile.

'Or will we live in England, so I can stay close to Kew and continue my work with Mr Banks and the Queen?'

Van der Humm's confidence returns. He walks across

the room, takes Daisy by the waist and looks deeply into her eyes. 'Why do you think I took the house at Brentford? Is living across the river too far from your beloved Kew?'

Daisy puts her hands on his shoulders. 'Indeed, it is not.'

Van der Humm puts his hand under Daisy's chin and lifts her mouth towards his. 'In which case, your answer is…?'

Daisy sighs, then looks him in the eye, silent for a few seconds. 'In that case, my answer is—'

There is a sudden, urgent knock on the door, and Kate enters wide-eyed. Van der Humm looks at her furiously. Daisy looks shocked. 'Yes, Kate, what is it?'

Kate is fearless. 'Excuse me, miss, The Viscount Minnella is here to see you, with another man… a Mr O'Flynn.'

Daisy's jaw drops, and she takes a small step back from Van der Humm. Rupert pushes past Kate, sees Van der Humm, and stops in his tracks. The man following him stops, filling the door-frame.

Rupert breaks the silence. 'Daisy, what in God's name are you doing? More to the point, what are you doing with *him*?'

As if she has just discovered she is holding something unpleasant in her hands, Daisy angrily pushes Van der Humm away. 'Rupert, we thought you were dead!'

Rupert is flabbergasted. 'Dead? Dead? Who told you that?'

Daisy now backs further away from Van der Humm,

pointing at him. 'He did!'

Van der Humm tries to make mollifying gestures. 'In God's name, I heard it in Liverpool.'

Rupert snorts in contempt. 'That man would tell you anything if it suited his ends. Has he told you that his preference in women is "black tulips" – the female slaves he imports not from Ireland but from your brother-in-law Hugo's estates?'

Emotions ranging from amazement to anger cross Daisy's face.

'And has he told you he is an agent for the Dutch government? And that his reason to be at Kew and to befriend you is to get close to Her Majesty?'

Daisy looks from one to the other before fixing her gaze on the Dutchman. 'Is this true, meinheer?'

Van der Humm shrugs. 'Believe what you will.'

'Well, meinheer, it seems there are a lot more questions other than simply where we might live that you would have to answer before I could agree to marry you. I think it is best you leave.'

Van der Humm glares at Daisy then swings a fist at Rupert. It never arrives. Quick as a cat, the dark-haired man with Rupert glides forwards, catches the hand in mid-air and twists it behind Van der Humm's back.

'I do believe the lady asked you to leave.' Daisy notices his accent has a definite twang. With the ease of a man controlling a puppy, he ushers Van der Humm out of the door and out of the cottage.

Rupert is distraught. 'Marry him! That is ridiculous. How could you be so foolish?'

Daisy looks away. 'Not so much foolish as fooled, perhaps.'

'It is one and the same thing! I thought you had agreed to wait until I returned?'

Daisy's cheeks colour. 'I agreed to no such thing. Why on earth should I wait for a plant hunter who criss-crosses the oceans and the continents to hither, thither and yon. How was I to know you would ever come back?'

'You believed me dead? I've never heard such rubbish – and from an educated woman too!'

'Everyone believed you dead!'

Rupert stares at her in stony silence, until she can no longer hold eye contact and looks away. Then he says through clenched teeth with faintly controlled rage, 'Well, *everyone* – was – *wrong*.' He shouts the last word at the top of his voice.

O'Flynn returns to the room, smiling, looks from one to the other and tries to break the tension. 'To be fair, Rupert, it was touch and go more than a few times.'

Daisy tries to deflect Rupert's anger by changing the subject. 'Have you been to see your mother? She believes you dead too – she is distraught.'

'No. I came to see you first, the moment I arrived. Although following this charade, God only knows why.'

In the corner, Kate is trying to supress a smile. Daisy's face softens. 'Well, she will be delighted that you are alive and well, and…'

Rupert has put his head to one side to look at her, and

Daisy suddenly realises this is something she has always found strangely endearing about him.

'And what, Daisy?'

He turns to O'Flynn and makes a dismissive wave of his hand towards Daisy. 'Come on, Dogget, we don't want to spend any time here, after all. I was mistaken – there are no friends in this room.'

Daisy puts her hands on her hips and juts out her jaw. 'And I am pleased that you are alive and well. Even if you are as stupid as ever!'

Rupert storms out. O'Flynn looks from one to the other, bemused. 'Pleased to meet you, Miss Salter.' He bows. 'Dogget O'Flynn at your service, delighted to make your acquaintance and hoping to have the pleasure again, in the near future.' He turns and follows Rupert.

Daisy collapses onto the sofa, puts her head in her hands and sobs. Kate sits next to her, wrapping her arms around Daisy's shoulders.

Outside, Rupert is pacing up and down the path as Dogget walks out of the door.

'Well, O'Flynn, what do you say to that farce?'

Dogget takes a cigar from his coat, lights it, draws on it and then looks at Rupert through the fragrant smoke. 'I say that I can see exactly why you were in such a hurry to get back – in fact, I'm amazed you ever left her in the first place.'

Rupert makes a harumphing noise. 'You're suddenly the expert on love?'

'I've been married and know the pain of loss only too well.'

'Yes. I had forgotten. I apologise.'

Dogget nods acceptance, takes another puff and sighs with satisfaction. 'Anyway, this is not about me, Rupert – it's about you. And I would say you have a bit of a fight on your hands. It may take more than a well-aimed shot from a long nine, but if any woman is worth fighting for, she's the one for you.'

IN A HEARTBEAT

The following day finds Rupert walking arm-in-arm with his mother, the countess, along the new Hollow Walk that Capability Brown finished the previous year.

Rupert regards the work approvingly. 'It has some way to go, Mama, but as I believe Brown himself would say, it has capabilities.'

The countess laughs. 'It is good to have you home, Rupert. I thought you were lost.'

They walk in silence for a moment. 'It wasn't exactly the homecoming I expected… You know I asked Daisy for her hand before I left, and asked her to wait for me?'

The countess looks surprised. 'No. I didn't. Why did you not tell us?'

'In case I didn't come back.'

'Have you asked her again?'

'Why? She was preparing to marry that scoundrel and liar Van der Humm.'

'She thought you were dead. We all thought you had perished. I know she asked the Queen's advice, and Her Majesty was of the opinion that she needed to marry and that Van der Humm's prospects and position made him very eligible.'

Rupert stops and turns to her. 'Would you and father think she was an eligible match for me? I am besotted with her.'

'There are better bred women – although there is nothing wrong with the daughter of a good baronetcy. There are better favoured and more elegant women – of course, beauty is as beauty does. There are women with considerable fortunes – not that money matters. Indeed, there are women who are all three.'

The couple resume walking. 'Whilst that is all very interesting, Mama, it does not answer my question.'

'What I did not say is that I have met no young woman who is more intelligent, more insightful, more talented, more honest about life or fuller of surprises than Miss Daisy Salter. It means, of course, that any man who seeks her hand would have to be prepared for a life full of surprises.'

Rupert is thoughtful. 'My friend, O'Flynn, says I should fight for her, that she is worth fighting for.'

It is the countess' turn to stop. She takes both of Rupert's hands in hers. 'I like your mysterious Mr O'Flynn. He is attractive, he is roguish, yet he is without doubt a gentleman. Above all, in his consideration of you and Miss Salter, I believe him to be most perspicacious.'

Rupert leans in and kisses her cheek. 'I'll take that as a yes then, Mama?'

'Well, she is certainly not going to marry Meinheer Van der Humm, of whom your father says there is no sight of hide nor hair, so she is free to choose. However, you still have to catch her, and if you take my advice, you will set about it with an intelligence equal to hers. She will not be wooed as other women are wooed with pretty words and politenesses. But if you apply both that big brain and your big heart to the matter, I think you'll work it out.'

The two walk back to the main gardens, chatting happily. As Rupert leaves her at the door of the Queen's cottage and turns to go, she stops him.

'Oh, Rupert, I almost forgot. Your father asked for you to call at his office tomorrow – he wants to welcome you back, and he says he has a task for you.'

That same night, Kate is brushing Daisy's hair as part of the pre-bedtime ritual. Candlelight flickers in the mirror. It is a warm evening, and the windows are open so they can hear a bird's song coming from across the gardens.

'Listen, miss, I think it is a nightingale.'

Distracted, Daisy finds she can't concentrate on the birdsong. She stops Kate's brush and turns around to look at her. 'Oh, Kate, I think I have been stupid.'

'There's not a single stupid hair on your head, miss.'

'I don't think a lot about men, but I am aware that I should find a husband, and I thought I might have a choice, and then I lost the choice, then I thought I had made the right choice, and now it seems I might have no choice at all.' A tear wells up in her eye. 'The thing is, Kate, every time I see Mr Fitzgerald, I feel my heart beating faster.'

Kate hugs Daisy to her bosom. 'Don't worry, miss. If Mr Fitzgerald is the right man, trust him to make the right choice. He'll choose you right enough.'

Daisy gives a wan smile. 'That remains to be seen. But tell me, how is your Mr Gardner?

'He's working here three or four days a week, miss, so I get to see him then... and sometimes, we find a place to be alone.' She giggles and puts a hand over her mouth. 'Often in a greenhouse. And, of course, we go to church together on Sundays.'

'You make life sound so simple, Kate.'

'A slave's life *is* simple, miss. But you wouldn't want to swap.'

'Would you want to be freed?'

'There is news that Lord Mansfield, the Lord Chief Justice, has just freed a runaway slave called Mr Sommersett, declaring that there is nothing in English law whereby one man can be another's property. That means there is hope for all slaves, miss. Although I am quite happy being who I am and where I am and doing what I do.'

'Good Lord, Kate, where did you get this information about Lord Mansfield?'

'The same as always, miss. It was in *The Gazette*.'

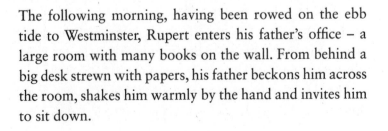

The following morning, having been rowed on the ebb tide to Westminster, Rupert enters his father's office – a large room with many books on the wall. From behind a big desk strewn with papers, his father beckons him across the room, shakes him warmly by the hand and invites him to sit down.

'Ah, you are well come, Rupert. I somewhat doubted you were dead – rather pleased you're not. It's good to see you.'

'You have more faith than some people.'

'Never did trust Van der Humm. Rogues have to be plausible liars. At least the King has a thousand tulips in his back garden.'

Rupert looks underwhelmed.

'We have kept close watch on him, you know. I didn't have the evidence to step in and stop him – but I may have it now. With your help, and perhaps that of your Miss Salter, I do believe we can nail your Edam-eating slave-trader.'

At this, Rupert sits up and sits straight. 'How?'

'Do you know anything about tea?'

'*Camelia sinensis*. Yes, of course. I'm a botanist and I drink it.'

'Specifically, different types of tea leaf? Suppose I had different types of tea, could you tell them apart?'

'Under a microscope, yes. Why?'

Clonmel walks across to a side table, unstoppers a decanter and returns with two glasses of port. 'There's tea trouble brewing in the colonies.'

'Is that a joke? The colonists can't brew tea properly?'

'What? No, sorry. The colonists don't like paying tax, and so the Dutch are profiting from smuggling their own tea in. Rumours are the insurrectionists plan to attack our clippers in Boston harbour. It could mean war.'

Rupert's father takes Rupert to a table on which stand four tea caddies. He motions that Rupert should take a look. The young botanist opens the canisters and sniffs the tea.

'Rupert, three of these are English, one is Dutch, intercepted in a shipment meant for a certain Dutchman of our acquaintance.'

'And you want me to prove there is a difference?'

'Do so and Meinheer Van der Humm will be hoist by his own teapot.'

Rupert smiles at the thought.

His father continues. 'In the meantime, if I can give you some fatherly advice, build bridges with Daisy Salter. I would much rather have a conversation with *her* over supper than any of those simpering women your cousins have married. Now, before you go, you must tell me about your adventure with that long nine – downing the mast first shot, never heard of such beginners' luck!'

Rupert bursts out laughing. 'No luck involved at all, Father. I was well taught.'

The earl claps him on the shoulder and fills their glasses. 'That you were, but I want to hear about every single moment.' He settles back into his chair as Rupert acts out the engagement in fine detail.

STRELIZIA REGINA

Spring also sees the King's retinue take up residence at Kew Palace. Having returned from visiting his father, that same afternoon sees Rupert, along with Banks, ushering a tall, carefully wrapped package, pushed in a wheelbarrow by two gardeners, up to the front steps where two footmen gently lift it out and carry it into the Dutch House at the Palace. Banks and Rupert follow them to a sunlit room where the King is sitting by a window reading papers.

Banks and Rupert approach the King who greets them with a wave of his hand as they bow to him – Rupert somewhat nervously. He takes a step backwards as Banks gestures to the package that has been placed on a low table.

'Your Majesty – I believe we may have met your request to discover a flower worthy of your queen.'

Rupert holds the plant as Banks unwraps it, revealing the magnificent bird of paradise flower displayed in a pot. The King walks over to examine it from all angles.

'Mr Banks, that is truly entrancing. It looks like a fantastical bird – wouldn't look out of place in the royal menagerie. What do you call it, Banks?'

'Your Majesty, it has no name yet.'

'Well, we can't have that – something this beautiful requires a beautiful name.'

He and Banks stand scratching their chins. Rupert looks hesitant but finally plucks up the courage to speak.

'Excuse me, Your Majesty…'

The King looks at Rupert recognising him for the first time. 'Young Minnella? Good God, man, your face is so tanned I took you for an under gardener. Should have known by the red hair.'

'I have been in the Cape of Africa, Majesty. And then at sea for some months. I am a little weather-beaten.'

Banks politely fills the ensuing silence. 'Indeed, Majesty, it was Mr Fitzgerald, along with Francis Masson, who discovered this plant on a hillside overlooking the Indian Ocean.'

The King looks from Rupert to the plant and back again. 'Good job, young man. Well done! Now, you were about to say something about a name for this stunning specimen?'

'Majesty, as it is a gift for the Queen, perhaps we should name it after her.'

The King looks bemused. 'Charlotte? Strange name for a plant, don't you think?'

'I was thinking of something more formal, Your Majesty, something that mentions her origins and her position as our queen.'

Banks nods encouragement. The King looks expectant. 'Well, tell us…'

'*Strelizia Reginae*, Your Majesty.'

The King walks around it, peering at it, stepping backwards to get a full view of it. 'Bit of a mouthful, but certainly regal enough. Can't we have a more popular name as well, Banks – can't see the flower sellers along Piccadilly getting their tongues round the Latin.'

'If I might, Your Majesty, you mentioned the royal menagerie at Tower Hill, and the flower does remind me somewhat of a pair of birds I brought back from the far east that are now installed there.'

The King regards him keenly. 'Yes, I remember now... What did we call them?'

'They are known as birds of paradise, Majesty.'

The King sits down and chuckles. 'Bird of Paradise. Yes, that would do nicely for my queen. But Banks, we must keep it secret until her birthday in a week's time.'

Banks and Rupert nod in agreement.

'Better still, gentlemen, I have an idea that we could play a small trick on her, for this plant is so fanciful, nobody could believe it real.'

He beckons Banks and Rupert closer and whispers to them.

Banks takes the plant back to the greenhouse, collects the two specimens that also survived the journey from the Cape and sets off to Daisy's cottage.

He expects Rupert to accompany him, but Rupert is nervous about seeing Daisy. 'I'm sorry, Joseph, but you must excuse me. I have a message for my mother from my father.' He strides off. Banks watches him and shrugs.

Kate is sent to fetch Daisy from her studio, and when she arrives, she finds Banks in her parlour with the three magnificent examples of the bird of paradise flower in their large pots. She gasps in delight.

'But these are beautiful, sir. Did Mr Masson discover them?'

'Mr Fitzgerald did. Mr Masson sent him back on the first available ship. They are to be named for the Queen – *Strelizia Reginae* – and gifted to Her Majesty on her birthday.'

'That is delightful, but why bring them to me, sir?'

Banks chuckles. 'The King has a plan. They are to be kept secret from Her Majesty, and all the world for that matter, until her birthday next week. You are to paint them, then he will give the Queen your painting as a flight of fancy. *Then* he will surprise her with the real-life flower.'

Daisy claps her hands in delight. 'The Queen will love that. It will be an honour to paint them. But I am to keep them here for a week?'

'Indeed. Now, they will need good care.'

'Mr Gardner, my sister's gardener, is at Kew. He could stay and tend them?

'Stay here?'

'His wife is my maid, sir.'

'Unusual, but yes. Can I leave that to you? Meantime, only those here and Mr Fitzgerald are to see them. Oh, and Mr Fitzgerald's friend, O'Flynn. Come to think of it, I will ask Mr O'Flynn to make sure he is here any time the gardener may be called away. He knows all about the plants having tended them on the voyage and is, shall we say, a useful sort of man to have around.'

Having seen the speed with which O'Flynn dealt with Van der Humm, Daisy nods her agreement.

UNDER THE MICROSCOPE

D aisy has set up her easel and is sketching the *Strelizia*, using her caliper for the exact measurements. There is a knock on the door, and Kate enters to announce that Rupert and O'Flynn have come to visit. Daisy flushes, feeling her pulse racing, then pulls herself together and motions to Kate to invite them in.

'Rupert, Mr O'Flynn, what a pleasant surprise.'

Rupert looks sheepish. 'We thought we would come and see how your work progresses.'

'And I have been detailed by Mr Banks to help ensure that nothing untoward happens to your plants – so I have come to see the lay of the land.' O'Flynn bows.

'You are most welcome, Mr O'Flynn.'

Daisy shows them the painting. 'It is a wonderful plant, Rupert. Where did you find it?'

'Dogget's guide led us to it. There were complete drifts of them in a field on a bluff overlooking the sea near the Cape.'

'The Queen will be amazed.'

The two look at each other in rather embarrassed fashion. O'Flynn sensitively slips out of the door. 'Just going to check the garden.'

Rupert breaks the awkward silence. 'I need some help. I left my microscope in the Cape. I know you have one—'

'Yes, it is in my studio. I can lend it to you. Why do you need it?'

'Tea.'

'Would you not be better using a kettle?'

Rupert grins. Daisy remembers she rather likes the way his eyes light up when he smiles. 'I have a project for my father. Your painter's eye might be useful. Please?'

Leaving Kate making tea for O'Flynn who is happy to stand guard over the plants, the pair repair to Daisy's studio.

They are taking it in turns to look through a magnificent microscope when the door opens, and Rupert's father walks in.

'Hello, Father! May I introduce Miss Salter.'

Daisy makes a curtsey, Clonmel bows politely. 'Miss Salter and I have already met briefly, at Bristol when I came to see you off.'

Rupert gives Daisy a look. 'You didn't tell me you were coming?'

'I was there with my sister seeing off her husband. We waved at you, but you didn't see us.'

Rupert looks pleasantly surprised.

The earl coughs. 'Anyway, I have heard a lot about Miss Salter and how talented she is'—he glances at Rupert—'albeit, mostly from my lady wife.

'Father, Daisy has lent me her microscope.'

The earl looks startled for a brief moment, but then nods to Daisy with respect. 'I had heard you were a scientist.'

'And botanist, Father – she has observed the different sorts of tea and produced large, detailed paintings of each sort.'

Daisy produces four paintings. 'I have scaled them up in proportion to be twenty times the size, and you can see, my lord that one of the specimens is quite different from the other three.'

Clonmel looks impressed and considers them carefully. 'This one is singular. Which is it?'

Rupert checks. 'Sample B, sir. Look, come and check through the microscope.'

The earl spends several minutes comparing slides on the microscope then nods his agreement. 'Without doubt, you have the right of it. Sample B is the Dutch sample. We have him! I will have him arrested. Perhaps you would like to join us and see what he has to say for himself?'

Having sketched the birds of paradise, and happy that she has the proportions right, Daisy is putting the final touches to her paintings. Gardner is fussing over the plants' care – watering them and spraying water on the leaves.

'Why do you do that, Gardner?' Daisy askes him.

'Mr O'Flynn says they grow facing the westerly breezes coming across the ocean, miss. So, they're bound to become used to the odd squall splashing them with water. I do believe plants are creatures of habit, or at least habitat, miss – I wouldn't want to do anything that kept them from what they're used to.'

'Mr O'Flynn sounds to have interesting ideas.'

He's an interesting man, that's for sure, miss. Something of a mystery about him, but no side to him – he's as happy to chat with me as you or Mr Fitzgerald. But my Kate has been the one to talk to him most. She says he's keen to discover more about his past.'

Intrigued herself by Rupert's friend and interested to pursue the conversation further, Daisy is interrupted by Kate announcing that Mr Banks and a visitor have arrived.

As Banks enters accompanied by a well-dressed gentleman with a beaky nose, Daisy jumps to her feet in delight and rushes across to grasp the visitor's hand. 'Mr Gainsborough. It's wonderful to see you. How are my dear friends, Mary and Meg?'

'My daughters are perfectly well, Daisy. But look at you – "Artist in Residence" at the renowned Kew Gardens. Mr Banks speaks most highly of you.'

Daisy beams. 'That, sir, is because you taught me so well. Why have you come to Kew?'

Banks butts in. 'Exciting news, Daisy – Mr Gainsborough has come to meet the Queen and talk about a portrait of the Royal Family.'

Daisy makes a mock curtsey. 'Well, there you have me, Mr Gainsborough – I have never taken much to painting people. I am still happy with flowers.'

Gainsborough is looking closely at the walls hung with many watercolour paintings of flowers. 'Painting flowers was where my mother started me off. However, I must say, Daisy, you are doing that remarkably well. What are these?'

He is pointing to paintings of various plants. 'Those, sir, are all paintings of plants named "Banksii" after Mr Banks, but these are just my preliminary sketches, not perfect. I have done better versions for the garden annals.'

Gainsborough looks straight at her and holds her gaze. Daisy feels as if she is being tested. 'Well, you must have a very critical eye. To me they are exceptional.' He looks to Banks. 'If they are not being used, might I have one for myself, and perhaps one each for Meg and Mary too?'

Banks looks at Daisy who nods. 'I am sure that will be possible. But I can't see why anybody would want a Banksii on their wall.'

Gainsborough selects three. 'I beg to differ, sir. Daisy, would you be so kind as to sign these for me?

'Sign them, sir?'

'Well, I sign all of my paintings.'

Daisy takes a brush, dips it in cerulean blue and neatly paints her initials.

Gainsborough is looking at the paintings of the *Strelitzias*. 'I don't suppose I could have one of those paintings?'

Daisy moves in front of her easel protectively. 'No, sir. I'm afraid not.'

Banks smiles. 'Not for all the money in the world.'

Daisy and Kate are settling into their familiar evening hair-brushing routine. 'Kate, Mr Gardner tells me he has learned much from Mr O'Flynn, and that you find him to be of great interest.'

'He's a lovely man, miss. Charming, with a gentleman's manners, but a bit sad as he knows nothing of his past. Like myself and Mr Gardner, he grew up on the plantations... but there's something quite different about him.'

She stops brushing, and Daisy turns around to look at her. 'How so, Kate?'

'It's as if he's got breeding, miss, like he's from some noble family. I met enough people on the plantations to spot the difference between the rogues and the chancers, and those who seemed to have a better will towards people in general. I'd say he's one of those, miss.'

She turns back to grooming Daisy's hair. 'All he has from his past is a document in a language he cannot read, and a locket with the faint portrait of a woman he supposes might be his mother.'

'That is quite fascinating, Kate. Do you know what he plans to do next?'

'Actually, miss, he asked me to ask you if you might help him.'

Daisy looks intrigued. 'Me, how so?'

'He has left me his document, miss. He thinks it is written in some European language and wondered if you might show it to the Queen, in case, being from Europe, she might know what language it is, or know somebody who does.'

Kate takes a yellowing folded document from her skirt and hands it over. Daisy carefully unfolds its leaves and studies it. The writing is in gothic style, the words running into each other as if the author was afraid of running out of paper. After a few minutes, she gives up.

'Frankly, Kate, it makes no sense to me at all. But I grant you it does look Germanic.'

'You'll show Her Majesty?'

Daisy nods. 'I will. I am due to visit the Queen at half past ten. Her Majesty enjoys a good puzzle.'

The Queen is in a petulant mood. 'The King is being most strange and mysterious. I asked him whether we should have a party for my birthday, and he simply told me to wait and see. What does he mean by that do you think, Madeleine?'

The countess is placatory. 'Perhaps the King is planning some surprise for you, Ma'am.'

The Queen looks scornful. 'A man, arrange a surprise with any sort of success! What are the chances of that, do you think? Let me tell you, he has two chances – a thin chance and a fat chance.'

Keen to take the heat out of the situation, Daisy, who knows the King's plan only too well, changes the subject. 'Your Majesty I have been asked by Mr Fitzgerald's friend, Mr O'Flynn, to request your help with something.'

The countess is quick to support her in changing the subject. 'What is it, Daisy? I'm sure Her Majesty will happily help a man who was able to captain a crewless ship and sail my son to safety.'

The Queen looks rather cynically from one to the other. 'I'm not fooled by you two, and I'm certainly not forgiving the King for his mysterious behaviour, but what is it he wants?'

Daisy takes the letter from her painting case, opens it, smooths it flat and passes it to the countess who hands it to the Queen who regards it curiously.

'Mr O'Flynn is the owner of this document?'

Daisy nods. 'It is all he has from his childhood. He hopes it may be a clue to who his parents were. He also has a locket, which contains a small miniature he believes to be of his mother.'

The Queen studies the document some more. 'I do not have the skill to read this…'

Daisy looks disappointed.

'But I know what it is. This is written in an Old Germanic code – it is the script they used to use for political and royal correspondence. If Mr O'Flynn owns this, he owns a document of some significance that needs to be properly deciphered.'

Daisy is sitting on her hands to contain her excitement. 'Majesty, is that possible?'

'Everything is possible when you are a queen! The King has one or two clerks who still use this script to send messages back to Hanover where the King is also ruler. It is intriguing. I will ask them to decipher it.'

The countess looks unimpressed. 'I hope it isn't just a merchant's inventory.'

'I think not, Madeleine. Daisy, be as good as to bring your Mr O'Flynn to see me tomorrow afternoon. And ask him to bring his locket with him.'

Daisy is strolling back to her cottage to share the news with Kate when she sees O'Flynn running towards her.

'Mr O'Flynn, I have good news…' She sees his shocked face and stops.

'Miss Salter, I have nothing but bad news. I went to your cottage to check on the plants and found your maid Kate bound and gagged.'

Daisy asks no more but runs towards her cottage with O'Flynn close behind. On arriving, she finds Kate sitting in the kitchen. Kate tries to stand up, but Daisy gently remonstrates with her to stay sitting whilst she describes what happened.

'It was the Dutchman, miss; he was here – crept up on me, gagged me and tied me up.'

'He has gone? And you are not harmed, Kate?'

Kate nods. 'Yes, miss.'

'Then we need not be too alarmed for now.'

'Except he barged through the door, saw the Queen's flowers on the table and ran off with one of your paintings.'

'No matter. I can easily paint another. Was anybody else here?

'No, miss.'

'Good. Mr O'Flynn, would you be so good as to walk at a good fast pace, don't run and attract attention, to Mr Fitzgerald's greenhouse, quietly share with him what has happened and then bring him back here? If you see Mr Banks, ask him to join us.'

O'Flynn nods and leaves, whistling, with his hands in his pockets – but at a quick march.

'In the meantime, Kate, not a word of this. Not even to your husband.'

THE ASPIDISTRA

S ome hours later, de Vries and Van der Humm are sitting in a riverside garden, drinking coffee.

'I admire your garden, meinheer. Although not typically of Dutch design.'

'I sometimes think, Johannes, that we Dutch are perhaps too rigorous in cleaving to our own style and could learn a few things from the English. Besides, it is still a lot tidier than the mess you have made at Kew.'

'Indeed, meinheer – although I hope I have found a way to redeem myself.' He reaches for his satchel and hands De Vries a rolled-up piece of paper. 'I bring news of a rather exciting discovery – a flower like I have never seen. It is unique, from the Cape.'

'Is it as good as a tulip?'

'See for yourself. It is fantastical – it looks more like a bird than a flower.'

De Vries carefully unrolls Daisy's painting, a slow, ever-broadening smile crossing his face. After some study, he looks up at Van der Humm, eyes twinkling, and nods his approval. 'So, Johannes, what is your next move?'

'I propose to annex the plants themselves and take them back to Holland for our own skilled gardeners to propagate.'

De Vries raises his cup in a salute. 'Annex? An appropriate choice of words as they are English property. It will be some small payback for the loss of New Amsterdam! Don't mess it up, and don't get caught. England has already had the War of the Roses – let us not get involved in the War of the Exotic Bird-Like Flower!'

'My thoughts exactly, meinheer. Could you perhaps put me in funds?'

De Vries throws him a purse that jingles with coins as Van der Humm catches it.

Having left de Vries' garden, happy with his lot, Van der Humm is strolling along the towpath with a spring in his step when three men jump him, put a sack over his head, bundle him into a carriage and drive off.

Also in a carriage, Rupert and Daisy are en route to meet the Earl of Clonmel. Rupert is more grandly dressed than normal. Around his neck, he wears a small, white, enamelled shield with a large red cross.

'Rupert. Who exactly is your father?'

Rupert looks at her, wondering whether to dissemble. He opts for the truth. 'He is the King's spymaster.'

'He seems far too nice and kind a man.'

Rupert grunts. 'Many foreign spies have made that same mistake.'

'Lucky for me then, that I am not a spy.' She points to the shield. 'What is that?'

'It is my family coat of arms. A badge of office for formal occasions.'

'Is arresting Van der Humm a formal occasion?'

'It adds weight to my evidence as a gentleman.'

Daisy looks out of the window. 'You didn't tell me you had a title.'

'Viscount? It's only a small one.'

'Should you marry, what title would your wife have?'

'Viscountess. At least until my father dies. Then I shall become the earl, my wife would be the countess, and my mother would become the dowager countess.'

Daisy waits for more, but Rupert says nothing, so she resumes looking out of the window as they ride through Knightsbridge, wondering what it would be like to be viscountess.

When they arrive at the earl's office, they find Van der Humm tied to a chair with the sack still over his head and guards on both sides. Rupert and Daisy remain standing, but the earl sits facing Van der Humm. He indicates to one of the guards who steps forwards and removes the sack.

'I must say, meinheer, it is something of an honour, albeit a rather dubious one, to meet a man of so many nefarious talents.'

Van der Humm can't resist a sly smile.

'Slaver, liar and seducer – all noxious things, yet none of which give me the authority to send you to the Tower. Almost certainly a spy – which I cannot yet prove. Burglar at Kew Gardens – although I only have the evidence of a maid. But now, I *can* prove that you are a smuggler! Which means I *do* have the authority to lock you up and then hang you.'

Van der Humm is nothing if not cool under pressure. 'I think my government would need to see unequivocal proof, sir, before they allowed you the latter option.'

Clonmel walks to his desk and picks up some sheets of paper.

'And here, meinheer, I have it. Paintings, sir, produced from scientific observation of tea leaves under a powerful microscope.'

Van der Humm is dismissive. 'They are but sketches made by a girl. They will not signify.'

Rupert is affronted by the Dutchman's complacency. 'I must correct you, sir. They are not sketches; they are in fact scientifically accurate representations. Miss Salter has now had the chance to compare the cargo of tea addressed to you with samples of smuggled tea seized in America. They are identical.'

Van der Humm shakes his head dismissively. 'Scientific or not, they are still made by a girl.'

'I am an earl of this realm, sir, and I would say, unequivocally, she is a lady. And one whose veracity of botanical likeness is trusted by not only the greatest scientist in the land, but also by our queen and, indeed, our king.'

Van der Humm hangs his head.

'Meinheer, you have nowhere to go in this argument… but the Tower.'

Van der Humm looks resigned. 'Very well, but I am

a gentleman. Free my limbs, and I will go with your men with dignity.'

Clonmel lets his men untie Van der Humm who stands up and walks towards the door. As he passes Daisy, he grabs her around the neck before spinning around to face the others. Rupert reacts most quickly, picking up a large flowerpot and crashing it on Van der Humm's shoulders, forcing him to let Daisy go. In the small space, the guards are finding it hard to get involved. Van der Humm wrestles with Rupert, rips the shield from his neck and pushes him to the floor in the path of the guards, tripping them up. In the melee, he takes the key from the lock, slips out of the door and swiftly locks it behind him.

Daisy, breathing heavily from having been manhandled, regards the broken flowerpot on the floor. 'My Lord, your poor *Aspidistra eliator*.'

The earl is red in the face. 'Bugger the aspidistra!' He brings his fist down hard on the desk. 'Bunglers! Well, he won't get far. We'll soon have him again.'

The following morning, as agreed, Daisy, accompanied by Rupert, takes O'Flynn to visit the Queen.

Rupert looks at his friend. 'You nervous to meet Her Majesty?'

'A little. But not so nervous as I was when you fired that cannon.'

'Nonsense. Even after that first shot, I still had plenty of balls.'

O'Flynn looks sideways at him. 'Yes, I'll grant you that.'

Rupert looks sideways at Daisy, but the comment has passed her by.

In the Queen's parlour, Rupert makes the introduction. 'Your Majesty, Mother, may I present my very good friend and travelling companion Mr Dogget O'Flynn who safely navigated me back from the Cape of Africa when we were in quite dire straits.'

O'Flynn makes the deepest of bows and stays low. 'Your Majesty.'

'Rise, Mr O'Flynn. The King and I both thank you for your service in bringing our loyal subject, the Viscount Minnella, safely home. Although, according to the document you had in your possession, that I have had translated, I do not believe you are really Mr O'Flynn at all.'

All eyes stare at the Queen, in bemused silence.

'Mr O'Flynn, would it be possible for me to see your locket?'

'Of course, Your Majesty.' O'Flynn undoes the top buttons of his shirt, takes the locket from around his neck and passes it to the Queen who opens it and stares at the image within for suspense-filled minutes before saying, 'I think you had all better sit down.'

Daisy, Rupert and O'Flynn do as they are told. The Queen brandishes O'Flynn's document.

'Interestingly, this concerns three of us here. You, certainly, Mr O'Flynn. But, also you, Daisy, and, remarkably, myself.' She hands the locket back to Dogget. 'Mr O'Flynn, it seems that you and I are related.'

There is a stunned silence. The countess has a mystified frown, Daisy's jaw drops, and Rupert regards his new best friend with a curious look.

Precocious as ever, Daisy is the first to speak. 'Majesty, I do not see how it can affect me at all?'

The Queen waves the letter again. 'Daisy, I do not know if you were ever told that the man, Godolphin, was married before he met your sister, that she is his second wife.'

'I had heard something, Ma'am. He took his wife and her son, by her own previous husband, to the colonies where they were deemed to have perished from a fever on one of his estates.'

The Queen looks stern. 'The lady in question was a cousin of mine whose first husband had tragically died when thrown from his horse in a forest. She came here with her infant son, met Godolphin and, needing a husband, married him. At that time, he legally adopted the son – I imagine he wanted the royal connection. It is she who wrote this letter. I believed the moment I saw it that it had to come from someone of royal blood.'

Rupert is on the edge of his chair. 'So, you believe that Dogget is Godolphin's adopted son?'

'I do not doubt it Mr Fitzgerald. The only question that remains is what happened to my cousin? I know they had been married for just over two years, and she had not conceived – I can only fear the worst and presume Godolphin simply got rid of her.'

Suddenly Daisy sits bolt upright. 'Godolphin, Your Majesty! And Dogget O'Flynn! Tell me, Mr O'Flynn, were you always called Dogget?'

O'Flynn is somewhat taken aback by all of this. 'To start with they called me Dog, but one of the overseers thought that too cruel. And I was a small lad so Dogget it became.'

'I thought so.' Daisy has their full attention. 'Dog O'Flynn, a derogatory name indeed for a boy. But reverse the word Dog, and you have God O'Flynn. Which is as close to Godolphin as any name I can imagine – it would be but a simple mistake for someone to make. Godolphin was their master on the plantations, but they couldn't bring themselves to kill a small child – albeit, Majesty, they may have killed his mother.'

The Queen once again regards the painting within the locket. 'More to the point, I think Godolphin may have killed his own wife, my cousin. Daisy, I am sad to say I am sure you have the right of it. This miniature, faint though it now is, looks very much like a family portrait I remember from my youth.'

There is stunned silence before the countess speaks. 'Daisy, do you know the whereabouts of your brother-in-law?'

'He was last seen sailing for his estates in the colonies, your ladyship. I think my sister expects him to return within the month.'

The Queen looks stern. 'When he does, I will see to it that the King has him taken immediately to the Tower. Whilst Godolphin's shady business matters may already be under the closest scrutiny, what we have discovered here is a capital crime. The man will hang for sure. Mr O'Flynn – as you now appear to be related to the Royal

Family, I will appraise my husband of the situation, and he will ask his advisers what the protocol should be. Now, leave me to think and consider.'

SKULDUGGERY

The following day, Rupert and Daisy are walking arm-in-arm, relaxed with each other, reflecting on the episode with Van der Humm.

Daisy looks at Rupert. 'I wonder where he is. I hope I never have to make his acquaintance again.'

'I feel exactly the same way. Although I must say I never thought I'd get the chance to save a girl's virtue with a pot plant.'

Daisy squeezes his hand. 'Gardner is re-potting your father's aspidistra. But thank you... and sorry I have been so mistaken about things.'

'You had imperfect knowledge.'

They walk on in companionable silence.

Rupert coughs nervously. 'Daisy, there is something I would ask you.'

The pair stop, and he turns to face Daisy. 'Daisy, Miss Salter—'

Suddenly, there is the sound of running feet and two uniformed sergeants rush up and grab Rupert by the arms. 'You need to come with us, sir – you are under arrest on suspicion of theft.'

Daisy is open-mouthed. Rupert struggles. 'What do you mean? Theft of what?'

The second sergeant points to Daisy. 'Plants from the residence of Miss Salter.'

Rupert struggles some more. 'I have done no such thing.'

The first sergeant holds up the enamelled shield Van der Humm had ripped from Rupert's neck. 'You deny this is yours, sir? It was on the table where the plants had been.'

Daisy remonstrates. 'Sergeant, it is his, but it was stolen by a Dutchman called Van der Humm.'

Rupert thinks on his feet. 'Daisy, the Dutchman is the thief. Quickly. You must make haste to Brentford – he will try for a boat. I will sort this mess out. Go! Now!'

Daisy takes him at his word, hoists her skirts and sprints to her cottage. Kate is waiting at the door with Gardner as Daisy arrives.

'Kate, I hear the plants have been stolen?'

'Not exactly stolen, miss.'

'What? That unscrupulous Dutchman has stolen the Queen's plants!'

Kate tries to speak, but Gardner stops her. 'Er, I gave them to him, miss. And helped carry them to his carriage.'

'You did what?'

He turned up here, miss, and said he was sent to collect them for the Queen's birthday – he showed Mr Fitzgerald's badge as his authority. Then he left it on the table.'

Whilst Daisy tries to take it all in, Kate continues. 'Then the sergeants came with some other men who had been instructed to escort the plants to the palace for the feast. They were very vexed to find them missing.'

'Did you not tell the sergeants the truth of it?'

'We tried to, miss. But why would they take a black slave's word? They jumped to their own conclusion.'

At that moment, O'Flynn arrives. 'I saw Rupert being escorted off by the sergeants. What is happening?'

Daisy holds him by the shoulder. 'Theft and skulduggery, Mr O'Flynn. I hear you're a good man in a tight corner.' O'Flynn nods. 'Very well, we must recover the plants ourselves. Follow me.'

Together, they rush into the courtyard where a carriage stands unattended. 'Mr O'Flynn – you can steer a ship of the line, but can you drive a carriage?'

O'Flynn jumps onto the box seat, puts out his hand and pulls Daisy up after him. Gardner takes the postern, and Kate climbs inside. 'Hold tight, Miss Salter!' O'Flynn cracks the whip, and the two horses break into a trot, a canter, then a half-gallop.

O'Flynn grins at the excitement. 'A bit faster than a ship of the line, Miss Salter. Where does your pleasure take you today?'

Daisy is hanging on as if her life depends upon it. 'Over the bridge to Brentford, driver, and don't spare the horses.'

O'Flynn cracks his whip again, and the carriage rushes harum-scarum across Kew Bridge, crashing through the toll booth and scattering pedestrians en route. At the far side of the bridge is a sign to Brentford, and the carriage makes a hard left. It continues up Brentford High Street until Daisy motions to halt in front of a tall house. O'Flynn pulls on the brakes with a loud screech.

Daisy jumps down, runs to the door and pulls on the bell. Gardner also jumps off. A black servant opens the door. Daisy asks him questions then walks slowly back to the carriage, head low, dejected. Gardner reaches the door just as it is about to close, thrusts his foot forwards and talks quickly to the servant. He then runs back to Daisy.

'Brentford Dock, miss – the Dutchman is planning his escape by boat.'

'Why did he tell you, Gardner, and not me?'

Gardener shrugs. 'He is my brother. All slaves are brothers and sisters.'

The carriage hurtles to the dock and comes to a halt by a ship's gangplank where crewmen are carrying on two tall packages under the anxious eye of Van der Humm who is holding a third.

'Stop, thief!' Daisy yells. Grabbing the whip, she jumps down and starts hitting Van der Humm.

He furiously sets down the plant, grabs hold of the whip and pulls her hard towards him. 'You again.' He scowls, grabbing hold of her. 'I hope you can swim, although if you sink so much the better.' He drags her towards the edge of the dock.

Daisy flings out an arm towards Kate who grabs it and starts pulling the other way.

'Hold tight, miss. We outnumber him; we'll save you.'

Gardner sees a nearby barrow of watermelons. He sprints over, and weighing them up for size, he picks the biggest and joins the fracas. Kate sees him ready for action and stamps hard on Van der Humm's booted foot. He yelps with pain, lets go of Daisy and staggers off balance.

In the distance, there is the noise of another carriage arriving. It's the royal coach carrying Rupert and the countess. As Rupert jumps out, Gardner throws the melon with force at Van der Humm who, off balance, catches it on his chest and tumbles into the water.

Kate rushes to congratulate her husband who looks disdainfully at the Dutchman struggling in the water. 'What a waste of a melon!'

Daisy walks towards Rupert. 'You're free!'

'Yes. The Queen saw the sergeants marching me off. My mother, out on an errand for her, picked me up, and we diverted the carriage here. Although we couldn't keep pace with you.'

Dogget has joined them. 'Nobody can keep pace when I'm driving!'

The countess catches Rupert's eye, and he leads them across to her. 'We must keep Her Majesty's flowers both safe and secret.'

Daisy looks around. 'Gardner and Mr O'Flynn can see to that, milady.'

Guards arrive, pull Van der Humm from the water and arrest him once again. He throws a contemptuous glower at Daisy and Rupert.

THE BIRTHDAY PARTY

With only a few hours to go until the birthday party, Daisy and Rupert, dressed in finery, are holding hands and making small talk with O'Flynn. Kate knocks and enters.

'Lady Fanny, miss, with her children.'

Daisy flies across the room as Fanny, carrying her new baby, hurries in with Esme clinging to her skirts. She is in tears.

Daisy addresses Kate. 'Take Esme to the kitchen and find something for her and the baby please.'

Kate takes the children and exits. Daisy hugs Fanny tightly. 'Sister, what on earth is the matter?'

Fanny breaks off, blows her nose and they all sit. 'It is Hugo. His ship was lost at sea. We are left alone, with no heir, so Hugo's beastly brother has thrown us out. Everything is lost.'

Rupert looks serious. 'I heard from my father that a slaver had gone down off the Fastnet rock – it must be the same ship. I am sorry, Lady Godolphin.'

Fanny looks surprised. 'Slaver – why was Hugo on a slaver?'

Rupert and Daisy exchange glances. 'Sister, there is

much you do not know about Hugo. We can explain in time. The first thing to do is get you settled – you and the girls must stay here.'

Dogget speaks for the first time. 'Miss Salter, I have not met your sister before, won't you introduce us?'

Daisy looks up at him and sees his eyes have come alight. 'Fanny, meet Mr Dogget O'Flynn, although we do believe he may soon, like you, be called Godolphin.'

Fanny struggles to take all this in, then stands to greet him. As their eyes meet and Dogget smiles, Fanny blushes all the way to her blonde roots.

Daisy is quick to note the mutual interest. 'Mr O'Flynn, meet my sister Fanny, the current Lady Godolphin.'

'Milady, this may be pure coincidence, or it may be fate.' He takes Fanny's hand and kisses it. He turns to Rupert and Daisy. 'I am not much for birthday parties. Should the Queen ask for me, which I am sure she will not, perhaps you can tell her I am caring for a damsel in distress.'

Elsewhere, a boat pulls up at an inn on a backwater tributary of the river. A figure emerges, tells the boatman to wait, enters the inn and raises an enquiring eyebrow at the innkeeper who points to a door at the back. The figure enters to find de Vries, dressed in black, sitting by the glowing embers of a fire. De Vries looks up, somewhat startled as recognition dawns on him. He indicates a seat and fills two glasses with red wine.

'Will you take a seat, my lord?'

'Thank you.' The first man sits down.

'Would you like me to take a drink of my own wine first Lord Clonmel, to assure you it is not poisoned?'

Clonmel picks up his glass and takes a deep draught. 'No need. They say there is honour amongst thieves – and I think that extends to spies.'

The man by the fire drinks deeply and raises his glass in salute. 'You are not who I expected.'

'Well, I wouldn't want you to drink alone, and as I have your usual companion in irons in the Tower, I thought I'd take his place.'

'I hope you will not mistreat him?'

'He'll be a bit uncomfortable, but for all he's a complete rogue, he's really quite likeable, and his only real damage has been to an aspidistra.'

The man by the fire smiles. 'He has not yet learned to care for plants.'

'It would seem so.' The earl twirls the stem of the glass in his hand. 'Do you want him back? Of course, he'd have to leave England and never return.'

'People like you and I, meinheer, we are always open to negotiation.'

The man in black takes off his spectacles, breathes on the lenses, polishes them with a cornflower-blue handkerchief, looks at each lens to see that it is clear, then wraps the wire legs behind his ears before pushing them back onto the bridge of his nose with the middle finger of his right hand. 'What might that cost my government? What would you ask us to do in return?'

'No financial cost at all, meinheer. And we would ask

you to do exactly nothing... or more to the point, to stop doing something.'

'Ah, this is to do with the Americas, I imagine?'

'Quite. We'd simply like you to stop trading in tea. Or at least, doing so at a price below the level of taxes we ourselves levy.'

De Vries considers. 'Perhaps we should persuade them to drink coffee instead?'

'Capital idea – we have no interests whatsoever in the coffee business. Can't see it ever catching on, but with the colonists, who knows. They are suitably uncivilised.'

De Vries looks thoughtful. 'What possible use could you have for Johannes Van der Humm? He knows no great secrets. For you he is another mouth to feed in the Tower. Another body to watch. Another body to bury.'

Clonmel remains silent. The pair regard each other across the table, like gamblers who are unsure whether to call a bet or fold. De Vries finally makes up his mind.

'Very well. If he comes back uninjured, we will take him back. Perhaps we will send him to America to open a coffee house.'

'As for the tea...?'

'As for the tea, we will dissuade God-fearing Dutchmen of the potential for profiting from tax-free trade. I cannot, however, legislate for privateers.'

Clonmel looks satisfied. 'Of course not. But I will accept your bona fides in this matter. Send note to me when you have a ship in the Pool of London, and I will have him delivered to you.'

De Vries nods his agreement, and Clonmel stands.

'In the meantime, let me thank you on behalf of the Crown for the gift of the tulips. My wife tells me they are magnificent. If you like, I can arrange for you to see them.'

De Vries rises from his chair. 'Thank you, my lord, but I cannot imagine any tulip field that can compare with my own beloved Keukenhof Gardens. I will politely decline.'

Clonmel looks him up and down. 'We are professionals, you and I, I do not find it out of the realms of possibility that in some matters we may be allies. Never hesitate to contact me if you feel we have mutual interests.'

He extends his hand. De Vries takes it warmly and the deal is sealed.

Back at Kew, Rupert and Daisy walk arm-in-arm towards Kew Palace for the surprise party.

'What are your plans, Rupert? For my part, I never want to leave Kew and my work here.'

'At some stage, I may have to become interested in my family's affairs in Ireland – but that is for the future. For now, I have found a house here overlooking the river and have agreed to buy it.'

'Is it a good house?'

'A good house and a big house. So for example, if I ever married, and my wife had family who needed a place to live, they would be welcomed. It would suit having children too.'

Daisy looks sideways at him as they walk on. 'That is kind, but I do believe my sister has a place to live.'

Rupert looks amazed. 'Surely, she cannot live with you

in your cottage… I mean, even if you were to leave?'

Daisy looks at him sideways again then looks straight ahead. 'No, I think she will be living at Godolphin House. The Queen has arranged that Mr O'Flynn – as he was – must be seen as the rightful heir to the Godolphin estate and take the title. He seems much taken with my sister Fanny, and she with him. In the short term I do believe he will invite her to live there, and they will come to an accommodation – she won't even have to change her name when they marry.'

Rupert takes his hat off and scratches his head. 'They will have to wait to ensure that brother-in-law of yours doesn't return from the dead like I did.' Daisy looks abashed but Rupert squeezes her hand and smiles fondly at her. 'By the way, I was going to propose to Godolphin's brother that I should buy both Kate and Gardner, and then employ them as freed souls.'

Daisy stops walking, reaches up and brushes him very lightly on the lips with hers. 'Except now, it is your friend, Dogget, you have to ask… I suppose he will still be known as Dogget? Anyway, he is quite capable of finding his own gardener, and Fanny will find a new maid and nursemaid when the time comes.'

Rupert puts his hand over hers where it sits in the crook of his elbow and the pair stroll on.

Kew Palace is sparkling for the Queen's birthday, and the guests are assembled around the royal couple sitting on their thrones. The King claps his hands for silence and signals to Banks and Rupert who carry across a large package. The King jumps down and removes the paper, exposing a magnificent painting of a *Strelizia*. The Queen steps down to examine it.

'My Lord, it is remarkable! Such a flight of fancy. Whose imagination is this?' Her eyes land on Daisy who makes a deep curtsey.

The Queen continues. 'It is a most surprising birthday present, my Lord. Well, it is like a unicorn. Or the bird of paradise that Mr Banks brought back from the East.'

The King is beside himself with delight. 'But there is more, my love. Shut your eyes.'

The Queen does so, Banks and Rupert bring in the flower, and the King whispers into the Queen's ear. 'Happy Birthday, Mrs King – you can open them now.'

The Queen opens her eyes and shrieks in delight.

Banks moves to the fore. 'If I might, Your Majesty? His Majesty has allowed me to name this plant, newly brought back from the Cape by the Viscount Minnella'—he indicates Rupert—'the *Strelizia reginae* in your honour.'

The Queen is beside herself with excitement. 'Mr Banks, Viscount... Your Majesty... I am delighted.' The assembled throng clap their approval.

Rupert wanders over to his parents and speaks to his father. 'Tell me, what became of the Dutchman?'

His father takes a sip from his glass. 'We gave him back to the Dutch...' Rupert raises an eyebrow. 'And you'd better, before you ask anyone why we have given something away, consider what we might have got in return. The Dutch will no longer smuggle tea into Boston – at least for the time being.'

Daisy comes and takes Rupert by the arm, curtsies to Clonmel and the countess, and walks him away into a corner.

'Daisy, it is a wonderful painting. It does the plant more than justice.'

Daisy curtseys, teasing him. 'Well, Viscount, I have another.'

'Is it just as magnificent?'

'Like your title – it is just a small one. Let us hide behind this plant, and I'll show you.' The pair take cover behind a massive potted aspidistra.

'Rupert, Viscount, before you left for the Cape, you asked me a question.'

'And...?'

'I have your answer.'

She takes from her bag a small piece of paper on which is painted a daisy chain. The space where, once, one daisy was missing, has been made complete.

About the Author

A self-confessed serotonin storyteller, Al Campbell wants the words he writes to make people happy. Writing is both a habit and a hobby – originally as an advertising agency creative director and copywriter, latterly as an MA student through flash fiction, short stories and poetry. In common with many creative people Al is dyslexic, something to which he attributes his love of dialogue. This is his first novel.

www.alcampbellauthor.com
@ACauthor
AlCambellAuthor
www.facebook.com/AlCampbellAuthor

Acknowledgments

Thanks to publisher Heather Boisseau for seeing merit in my manuscript when twenty agents (and counting) did not. She and her RedDoor team – Lizzie, Clare, Kat, et al. – made it a good tale, better told. Thanks to Clare Shepherd for the stunning cover design.

I owe early improvements to Dave Swan, my MA tutor at Chichester Uni, who showed me how to tighten my ramblings. You wouldn't have read this unless Bob Schultz of London Screenwriters Festival told me to convert my screenplay into a novel. Thanks to screenwriter and mentor Darren Rapier, who made me sit down and make the structure work right from the start.

Thanks to many others for the insightful advice that made me think things through in more granular fashion. Thanks to John Aparicio for the photography and video work. Especially, thanks to my in-house 'Daisy', who paints both the minutiae of wonderful flowers and large expressive abstract landscapes as Fleur Cowgill. When it got tiring, she kept me positive with courgette cake and malt whisky.

All things considered, whilst a lot of the early advice was from men, it took women to breathe life into the final delivery. I guess that's the nature of things.

IF YOU ENJOYED READING
THE DAISY CHAIN YOU MIGHT LIKE
TO KNOW ABOUT THE JOSEPH BANKS CENTRE

Sir
**JOSEPH
BANKS**
Society

The Joseph Banks Centre is in Banks's home county of Lincolnshire, located in a 17th century Grade II listed building in the historic town of Horncastle. It houses the Sir Joseph Banks Society, which runs and maintains the unique Joseph Banks tribute garden and plays host to the new Lincolnshire Herbarium, together with the historic Seaward Herbarium. It also focuses on Banks's impact in Lincolnshire and nationally, and through him our close links with Australia, New Zealand and the Indian Pacific regions.

Its collections and unique garden are visited by local interest groups and attract hundreds of tourists each summer. On a wider front, the society has an international membership and sits at the centre of a large network of Joseph Banks academics from across the world.

For more information and to learn how you can become involved please visit www.joseph-banks.org.uk

Alternatively email enquiries@joseph-banks.org.uk